Signs of Life

Signs of Life

Amy Head

TE HERENGA WAKA
UNIVERSITY PRESS

Te Herenga Waka University Press
Victoria University of Wellington
PO Box 600 Wellington
teherengawakapress.co.nz

ISBN 9781776921140

A catalogue record is available at the National Library
of New Zealand.

Published with the support of

ARTS COUNCIL OF NEW ZEALAND *TOI AOTEAROA*

Printed in Singapore by Markono Print Media Pte Ltd

... I say this in a city living in memory and expectation, in ghost streets and dream buildings.

—Elizabeth Knox, Ōtautahi Christchurch, 2014

I'll let you be in my dreams if I can be in yours.

—Bob Dylan, 'Talkin' World War III Blues'

Contents

Biographical Details

Before the earthquakes there would have been no good reason for the shipping container waiting in the driveway of Bette's new unit. She'd been staying with her daughter and son-in-law, north of the city, for the past year, during which time the assessors had decided she couldn't move back into the house she'd shared with her husband for forty years. It was blue, the container, and battered—the paint scratched and the steel dented in places. She could still read the company's logo and acronym on the side, not that the letters meant anything to her. There were similar containers all over the city nowadays. People cut holes in the side and sold coffees out of them. There was an entire mall in containers. Containers lined the road around the base of the cliffs to catch falling rocks. Bette had watched a scene in a sitcom where a character walked into a room that was decorated in an outmoded style and said, 'Did the seventies throw up in here?' The same character might drive through their city and say, 'Did a ship throw up around here?'

The settlement where Bette's daughter Bronwyn lived with her husband was dominated by the state highway. It stretched for a kilometre of shops and businesses and went two or three streets deep on either side of that, laid out on a grid with wide verges, almost wastefully so. Every week, Bette walked from their house to a café near where Bron worked, to have lunch. She usually passed someone from the pharmacy or real estate office holding a takeaway tray. That was what the people in the businesses did; they went back and forth along the highway availing themselves of each other's services.

Bette was usually early. On this particular day it hadn't yet gone twelve. From her usual table beside the window, she watched the counterhand tend to a squealing jug of milk. She shared the room with a trio of mothers and pushchairs. The server delivered Bette's coffee just as Bron opened and closed the door. 'Did the builder get hold of you?' She was tanned and scrawny. She parked at the end of farm access roads and went for long runs up hills. She pulled out a chair opposite Bette. 'He called early, before you were up. Sent you a text, apparently.' The unit Bette had bought needed repairs before she could move in. She reached for her handbag, on the ledge beside the window, and rummaged inside it for her phone. 'He said someone came to the door yesterday,' Bron added. 'A photographer.'
'What for?'

What Bette considered her most significant upheaval was not the earthquake itself, but having to shift out of the home she and Leo had brought the girls up in. In some respects the move had been more difficult even than her husband's death, several years earlier. Each room had been populated by familiar objects—shelves cluttered with albums, cookbooks and fossils they had walked upstream in the Waipara River to find, just the two of them, under the willows, in the push of the sparkling water (time after time it had undone her shoelaces), until eventually they saw the concretions, like extra-terrestrial eggs, emerging from a bank high above them. Most of their possessions had been redistributed by now. Some had been destroyed. Some Bette had lost track of.

Bron moved her chair closer. Bette opened the text and clicked on the link, which took her to what must have been some kind of website, but it wasn't easy to see on a small screen. The site looked commercial, a brand she thought she recognised from somewhere. There was a world map with plotted lines, but the world was too expansive for her screen. She could only view sections of it at a time. 'What's this for?'

Bron leaned in. 'Can I have a look?' Bette handed the phone over. Bron swiped the screen until she reached a series of photographs. Behind her, one of the mothers passed a marshmallow to a tiny hand that waved from its pushchair.

'What's IBC World?' Bette asked.

'They're a shipping firm.' Bron zoomed in. 'Mum. That's your place.'

Bette studied the image until she finally recognised the pots Bron had helped her to line up in front of her little unit—the geraniums were blooming. 'Why?'

'A news site has been tracking the container, look. It carried whiteware from Shanghai to Lyttelton, and before that, wine from California.'

The photographs showed a container (the same container?) sitting in port, suspended from a crane, conveyed on the bed of a truck, and now outside someone's home. Her home. 'What for?'

'For a granular view of trade, they say.' Bron scrolled across the images with her thumb. 'These all link through to different articles.' Bette couldn't read the titles—not at that size, not at that speed. 'Modern Piracy,' Bron said. 'Migration Hotspots.'

'Which am I, a modern pirate or a migration hotspot?'

'Current port, Lyttelton. See, "Disaster Recovery", they're still writing it. Didn't anyone tell you?'

'I don't think so.' Leo would have enjoyed this—tracking the container's route across the blue expanse, so broad it took several swipes to reach the next continent.

The shipping company said they would waive the cost of container hire. They wanted her to provide basic biographical details such as her age, family and occupation, and describe how she had been affected by the disaster. What was stored in her container and why? She was asked to supply a recent photograph of herself.

This news brought on a barrage of text messages from her granddaughter Felicia, or Flick. Gran's container had thousands of likes! Flick's friend was a photographer. He would take the photo. They arranged to meet at a café in the city—one of the first to reopen since the cordons had shifted back. Between the car and the footpath Bette had to pick her way over stones as big as her fist. She could still sense the pre-quake city, hovering just out of reach. Somewhere nearby there had been an Indian restaurant. Inside, all of the tables were full and the coffee was strong. Flick's company also had a quickening effect. 'You look nice,' she told Bette. 'Good hair.' Bette had let Bron talk her into getting her hair done. The stylist had been waiting for her with a round brush in one hand and a hairdryer in the other. The familiar scent of hairspray. Fixative laced with fragrance. Twenty-first birthday party. Graduation. Wedding. For the first time in ages she had stood in her slip and ironed a dress to wear.

'How's work?' she asked.

'My boss is selling up, as-is where-is.' Flick's hair was thick and curly. There was a green clip in it doing nothing, holding on for dear life. 'But the buyers offered me an office job, at a different site, doing production.' She had dropped her university papers for reasons Bette hadn't quite grasped.

'That's good, isn't it?'

'I guess so. What's happening at Donmar Street?'

'They've ordered a report from another structural engineer.' Her family home was now one of thousands of strays littering the city, boarded up and engulfed by weeds. 'I'm not holding my breath.' Bette didn't bother to go into detail—Flick was staring over her shoulder.

'This is Gran,' Flick said. 'This is Luke.' Bette recognised him from Flick's school days, but he'd become a man in the meantime.

'I remember,' he said. 'So you're my model today.' The top few buttons of his shirt were undone.

'I also answer to Bette. Thanks for your help.'

'He's usually in town taking photos anyway,' Flick said.

He positioned Bette at a table beside the window. Flick stayed behind. 'Cloud cover's good.' He adjusted his camera's settings. Bette gazed out at a three-storey façade across the street. It was supported by a steel frame and very fine, a heritage building. The café itself had been a post office, once upon a time. When Luke finally looked up, he was only interested in surfaces. He didn't meet her eye.

'Shall I smile?' she asked.

'If you like. Let's try both.' She faced the lens directly and held her hands in her lap. School photo. Hockey team. Staff ID. When she'd met her husband she'd worked in the office at a clothing factory. They made undergarments, mostly. Luke brought the camera up to his face quickly, almost apologetically, pressed the shutter button a few times and checked the display. 'Okay, this will work.'

'Wasn't that it?'

'A couple more.' She could hear the coffee grinder measuring out portions. Tap tap. They were drawing glances from the tables nearby. 'I remember going to your house when we were kids,' Luke said. All of five or six years ago, Bette thought.

'That house is a touchy subject at the moment,' she said. 'I've bought a small unit I'm moving into soon.'

'Sit tight there for a sec.' He was wearing deodorant or

aftershave; she was too much out of practice to distinguish. This conjured another set of associations, different ones altogether—whiskers, the warm hollow of a neck. She redirected her attention to the chalkboard propped up on the counter. The first option was *Typical porridge*. She read it again, *Topical porridge*. Again. *Tropical porridge*. Tropical porridge.

All she would carry with her was what was in the container, including her husband's best specimens, spread out among several boxes to distribute the weight. He had found his escape from her and the girls in his shed. This might be her escape now. That was the answer to the shipping company's question. What was in the container? Accumulation. Her most important memories, protected.

'I'll just scoot forward a bit,' Luke said. He took a few more shots, sat back from the table and busied himself with the camera again. Flick was bent over her phone, back at the table where they'd started. She and Luke seemed to have an unthinking ease with one another, as though they still spent a lot of time together. Flick wanted to bring him with her. Was that it? Not leave him behind, in the time before the quakes. 'Here,' Luke said. He held the camera out to show her. 'One of these I think.'

He pressed the arrow to run back through the sequence. Her former hockey player and graduate selves would have been appalled to see this version, with loose skin and grey hair. The unsmiling photos suggested that disaster recovery was a serious business, the smiling ones that she was staying positive. He'd cleverly captured some rubble in the background outside the window. A joke about fossils occurred to her, but she held it back. She looked neat and tidy, which was good enough. She didn't linger before mirrors or photographs anymore.

'Let's go with the smile,' she said.

Electrosmog

When Flick heard the counter bell ting, she was watching the AC1000 staple calendars into alternating piles. The receptionist hadn't started yet, so she left the machine to go about its task. After working under the LEDs, she took a moment to adjust to the rush of daylight. The customer was old, seventies or eighties, but his eyes were clear, and his gaze so direct it was almost rude. 'Hi,' she said. In a customer service webinar they'd been steered away from asking, *Can I help you?* Too clichéd, too little humanity. He didn't answer. She waited while he lifted a neat leather satchel onto the counter between them, and began to unzip one of the pockets.

She'd never seen so much white hair before. Actually white, not grey—white like a Samoyed or snow. She waited in stand-by mode while he eased the zip around its corners, unlocking teeth one by one. He was wearing a watch, the kind with metal chain links. 'What can I help you with?' she asked. He pulled the compartment open and looked inside.

'Oops,' he said. 'Wrong one.' She thought she caught a hint of an accent. He increased his speed to zip the pocket up again. With the same hand he gave the satchel what looked like an affectionate pat, then another in a different place, as if he were encouraging it to give up its secrets. Outside the front windows, across the road, was the façade of the old electricity substation, its bricks held up by steel struts.

Through the open door behind her, she could hear one of the printers in the back room churning, cleaning itself. There was still some resistance beneath the wrinkles on the customer's face—the bone structure of a large head. He had developed a new theory and started in on a different zip. Her anticipation wasn't quite so keen this time. 'Have you got a sniffle?' he asked, without looking up. She did, in fact. Her nose had been running all morning.

'Excuse me,' she said. She reached for a tissue.

'Hear that?' he asked. The roller door in the loading bay was letting in a faint trilling. 'That's a grey warbler.' His accent defied geolocation. He started in on another zip, one that opened into the main body of the satchel this time. 'Ah,' he said.

For half a second they heard a distant rumble. There wasn't time to react before the shaking started, as though a colossal finger had landed on their geological turntable, dragged them back a few degrees and let them go. The customer pulled his hand out of his satchel and gripped the counter. Flick eyeballed the substation across the road. Familiar spike of tension in her veins. A beam in the ceiling creaked once, twice, and the juddering stopped. The customer plunged his hand back into his satchel and lifted a book out. *Whump*, went the book on the counter. The strip light swayed on its cords. 'There,' the customer said. 'I need a copy of this, spiral bound.'

A hardcover with a dust jacket. The text was in a different language. She indicated the laminated notice on the counter. 'There might be a problem with copyright laws.' She couldn't tell if the faint swimming sensation under her feet was real or imagined. He pulled the book over. 'You probably knew that already,' she added. He leafed to the imprint page and spun it back around for her to see. 'Here.' He jabbed at the copyright line with his finger. Grigory Petrov. 'This is me.' It might be a history of vacuum cleaners. He could be lying. Still, he'd taken some trouble to get there, through mazes of traffic cones, negotiating road closures.

'Have you still got the files?' she asked him. 'You could email them to us.'

He shook his white head. 'No such thing as Word files back then. Anyway, people can steal digital files,' he said. 'To get their hands on a hard copy they'd have to come and find me.' He flipped the cover closed and pushed the book back.

Flick's manager emerged from her office. She'd probably had the same big hair for decades. She could tell you the GSM of a piece of paper by feel. 'Good rumble,' she said. 'Four point five.'

'Are the unions still strong around here?' The customer directed the question at Flick's manager, as though she'd been there all along.

'They used to be,' the manager told him, 'when Dad was

still here.' She'd put toast on in the kitchen. In wafted the smell of something that would melt butter.

'I'll be back Friday.'

'Do you need a quote?'

'No.' He picked up his satchel and that was that, he was gone, letting in road noise as he went.

Flick's manager picked up the book and weighed it in her hands. 'Last week it was the *Journal of Soviet Anthropology*.'

Flick programmed the alarm later that evening while the printers slipped off to sleep. She crossed at the intersection and entered the bar in the motel on the corner. They were only a couple of blocks from the inner city cordon and there were very few places open. She walked past the bartender, who was all spiked hair and motel logo, and sat in a booth near the tank. She watched a small fish, a flash of petroleum with an orange tail, dart out of a plastic shell and ambush another one the same. On the bottom, towards the back, was something else, an inky undulation. A rare pedestrian passed through a pool of streetlight outside the window.

The bartender put a glass of house red down in front of her. No, it wasn't the first time she'd avoided going home. 'Have you been at work?' he asked. He was a recent arrival from Dunedin—a disaster tourist, possibly. 'It's not good for you, all that electrosmog. We're exposed to enough of it already.' No one local was worried about electromagnetic anything, not at the moment. 'That big one's a catfish,' he said. 'They're good for keeping the tank clean.' The black shape had emerged further into the light. Now she could see white stripes and spines sticking out around its mouth. She simultaneously found his tone patronising and wanted to know more.

'What are they?' She pointed at the blue and orange ones.

'Neon tetra. They school together, see?'

'Not for long,' she said. 'They can't go anywhere.'

'They don't know any different.' He took the tea towel out of the pocket of his apron and spun it into a whip. Her phone buzzed on the table. It was Luke, her ex. Mostly ex.

Flick lived in an old workers cottage not far from the print shop. The suburb was semi-industrial, but several streets were named after writers and philosophers. People got their cars upholstered on Burke. A company on Byron manufactured plastics. The nights were long and the mornings loud. Inside on the couch, she paused before the TV without switching it on. She held the stare of the black hole. 'Not very pacey, is it?'

Flick jumped. Her flatmate, Renee, was behind her. 'Don't do that!' Flick said.

'The door was open.' Renee dropped herself onto a beanbag and looked over from her fanned layers of fabric, her face framed by wisps of hair. The effect was disingenuous. She wasn't wispy or ethereal. 'Feel that shake today?'

'Yeah.' A garage door clattered down on the other side of the road and a truck signalled that it was reversing. Signalled to no one.

'Luke might come over.' Flick said.

'So what else is new.' Her flatmate shifted her weight,

swamped in polystyrene.

'Have they caught the tarantulas yet?' They had escaped from the biology lab.

'I haven't heard. Have you decided whether you're coming back?' Lectures had started up again, or some of them had, in hastily arranged new venues, tents in some cases. According to one of the counsellors at the student health centre, what Flick was doing was reassessing her goals in light of recent events.

'Don't know.'

'You need some of those soft skills. The robots are coming.'

Later, she floated in a wary tilt of oncoming dreams, unable to feel her body, barely aware of what Luke was saying in his stream of talk, until eventually he lapsed into silence. She sensed that he was waiting for her to respond. 'Beware the electrosmog,' she told him in a thick voice.

'What?'

'The robots are coming.'

It was Thursday night when she finished copying the Russian book. She bypassed the bar, walked home, texted Luke and got into bed. At one in the morning there was an aftershock. Until three she was fully alert, in a stare-off with the stippled ceiling, reassessing her goals. When she woke again later, she baked for a while in the strengthening sunshine and wished evil on whoever was idling their engine outside. By the time she got to work the customer had already come and gone. In the kitchen, she watched her manager separate the two halves of an English muffin. 'He likes to be early,' her manager said. If the aftershock had compromised the structural integrity of her hairstyle, it wasn't obvious. Neither of them was in a particular hurry. The receptionist was at her station.

'So you know him?' Flick asked.

'Before last week I hadn't seen him in ages.'

'How long has he been coming?'

'Years. Decades, even. He used to deal with my father.'

'No one needs that much stuff copied.'

'Things were different back then. Hard copy was king.' Flick's manager jammed the lever on the toaster up, again and again. 'He was sent here in the sixties, Dad said, as a kind of training thing.'

'What kind of training?' Flick asked.

Each time the muffin jumped, her manager tried to catch it. 'It probably doesn't matter anymore,' she said.

'What doesn't?'

She caught one of the muffin halves and put it on a plate. 'He worked for the Russian government. He was only junior but he was in the intelligence services.'

'The intelligence services. And he just told your Dad about it.' This was obviously bullshit, but it was a weird joke.

'Well, that was the point. He wasn't very good at it. They drank together. He was careless.' Her manager caught the other half of the muffin and put it on a plate for Flick. 'He brought a map of Christchurch in with Cyrillic labels on it for Dad to copy one day.' A weirder and weirder joke. 'If you tell anyone I'll say it's made up.'

23

'Yeah, because you did just make that whole thing up.'

'Exactly.' They regarded each other. They took bites of muffin.

'He didn't write that book, then,' Flick said.

'I doubt it. Is that what he told you?'

'To get around the copyright.'

'I don't think they'll find out,' her manager said.

'Nah, I don't either.' Even if they did, it was a long way to come. The kitchen had only a small window, but Flick could see cars plying back and forth outside. 'So why do you think he's copying all that stuff?'

'I don't know. Because he wants to feel useful?' In the toaster, their second muffin shrank back on itself as it heated. The ground felt solid underfoot. Flick wasn't fooled though.

Someone to Heart-Emoji

Carla's daughter helped her with her dating profile. They were couch-side at home, sharing her laptop. 'I don't like this one,' Carla said. 'Too squinty.' It had been taken in the sand dunes not far from where she lived. She was looking into the sun.

'Don't get hung up on the photo,' her daughter, Skye, said. 'Pass me your glass. You've put meditation down as a hobby?'

'Is that a problem?'

'Hmm.'

'Would *threesomes* be better?'

Skye held her hand out. 'Give that back. No more wine for you.'

Skye had been raised on memes and YouTube channels. That was why Carla had finally succumbed to her urging, and to the technology that would, in theory, find her a life partner, someone to '♥'. Skye clicked on a profile. 'What about him? He's a surveyor. He plays disc golf.' She turned the laptop to give Carla a better look. His face was long. He was wearing glasses. Not smiling or squinting, just head-and-shoulders against a blank background, no mountains or city or anything.

'He looks a bit—strait-laced,' Carla said.

'His favourite movie is *Close Encounters of the Third Kind*. You made me watch that.' When Carla was Skye's age, she'd been dancing off hangovers and driving all night to festivals on the banks of West Coast rivers. She hadn't been managing her parents' personal lives. First came the festivals, then the soft swamp of cloth nappies and pastel jumpsuits.

He was late. Carla waited in the beer garden near the Arts Centre, where a band played every Sunday afternoon. Places like this, where there was no risk of falling concrete, had become popular since the quakes. This week's musicians were Argentinian or Chilean, maybe—millenials with tans and coloured wristbands. Carla moved the used ashtray in front of her onto the next table. A man in the booth opposite was looking over. He was bearded and wearing a suit. When she'd arrived her gaze had slid over him without stopping. Now he leaned forward. 'Carla?'

He'd been clean-shaven in his profile pic. Once Carla had settled into the booth, she homed in on the sharp cheekbones and grey eyes. 'What have you been up to?' she asked him. 'Have you come from work?' They had already performed their first negotiation: should he join her or should she join him? The concept of a man and a woman sitting at a table together was completely mundane, generally speaking, but not for Carla, not when she was the woman.

'Actually, I've been at a memorial service,' he said.

'Oh, I'm sorry. Were you close to the person?'

'He was the uncle of my ex-wife. My ex-uncle-in-law, I guess you'd say.'

'Okay. You must have known him quite well.' His beard concealed the bottom of his face. That was the difference. His face was cropped.

'Sorry, I shouldn't have—I know that's a downer. I didn't know him that well but we try and stay on good terms, you know.' He gulped back beer.

'Sure, I get it.'

He put his glass down, half empty. 'How about you?'

'Well, I went out on my boogie board in the morning.' A toddler ran along a strip of cobblestones between two sections of tables. The boughs of an oak reached over the back fence.

'Nice,' he said. 'Sounds good.' All of his speech had a strangely equivalent tone. He was having a horrible time and wanted to leave, was what that probably meant. Face-to-face was difficult—conversation with the potential for nudity. Suck it up, she told herself. Box on.

'Hey,' he said. 'Funny thing happened at work last week. Well, not funny exactly. They uncovered all these old bottles at the site where I'm working. It's been happening a lot, apparently. We have to step back and give the archaeologists access.'

'So what else have they found? Do you know?'

27

He put his glass down, finished. 'Mainly the bottles, and broken bits of crockery.'

'Why did people throw crockery away?'

'They used to dump rubbish in the river, too. Actually,' he leaned in, more enthused. 'All kinds used to drain into the Avon. Kitchen scraps, heaps of stuff.'

'So it's all under there now?'

'The stuff that doesn't break down I guess.' That was it: the moment when she knew for sure that he didn't have sex on his mind. When he moved on to talking about boxed timber culverts, she began to visualise her porch and a pot of tea.

For their next mother-daughter 'date' (Skye's term), they hired paddleboats. At first the river ran behind the hospital, alongside car parks and service entrances, but the scene soon became more picturesque. They paddled past lawns and a band rotunda. Their legs were occupied, but Skye still had the use of her hands. 'How about this one? He's a DOC ranger who's into home brewing and world cinema.'

'*World* cinema. So, not American?' Carla dipped a hand into the river, which hustled and rippled in its courses.

'I guess.'

'I'm not in a big hurry to link up with someone right away.' It was peaceful on the water, peering into the layers of green, at least it was when they stopped paddling and let themselves drift. They passed an envious curly-haired toddler and Labradoodle watching from the gravel. She'd never pictured her own city as Victorian, populated by buxom women in layers of aprons and skirts, pouring out their buckets of slops.

'I'm glad we got you out,' Skye said.

'You make me sound like someone's old mum.'

'You are.'

'Did you know the city's wastewater used to flow into this river?' she asked.

'Like what?'

'Kitchen scraps, heaps of stuff.' She should have met him here in the botanic gardens, or at the beach in the salty wind, not at the pub.

The company Carla worked for did work-station assessments, mainly for medium to large businesses. She'd originally trained as a physiotherapist but had developed repetitive strain injury in her wrists. At high school she'd been a gymnast. Her body had performed for her, once. The first time she'd landed a backwards somersault her legs had stretched out to meet the sprung floor and her feet had found it. Here I am, the floor had said. *Here*. Like magic.

Her last job the following week was the kind she didn't have very often—a private client, working from home. He lived on a street between a private school and a shopping mall. The house was brick, semi-detached. There was a single car parked in the driveway. He let her in and led her past a peace lily, woven wall hangings and painted masks to the small room he was using as an office. 'I'm under contract with a company in Adelaide,' he said. 'In the past all of this would have been done for me at the office. I've probably developed some bad habits.'

She had him sit at his desk and type. 'I'm quite sore here,' he said, and pressed into his trapezius.

'That's very common.' Neck and shoulder tension was public enemy number one, and it wasn't all down to faulty ergonomics. The people of the city were storing a lot of stress. 'You're lucky,' she said. 'You can use the mirror on this wardrobe to check your angles.' He knew it all already. He had the micropause software. He just needed reminding. She gave him the brochure with the stretch diagrams. 'Some people use oil burners,' she said. He didn't seem the type. 'Some people get a massage once a month.' He looked at her more intently, then. Oh God, she thought. What if he's seen my dating profile? He could be on the same site. He was in his fifties, give or take. He looked like anyone else. He had eyes, a nose and a mouth. Shoulders, hips and feet. His favourite movie could be *The Sound of Music* or something with James Bond.

'Is that a service you provide?' he asked. 'Massage?'

She told Skye about it on date night. Dinner and a movie. 'It says so on the company's website. After my name it lists my qualifications, including my massage diploma.'

'So he read your individual profile? That's creepy.'

'If it's so creepy, why do we have them?'

'I don't know, but it is.' A server came with their noodles. Her top was the colour of a fluorescent melon but she looked tired. Skye asked, 'What did you tell him?'

'I told him I don't do it anymore.'

'No kidding you don't. Back off, Harvey.' Skye stabbed her pile of noodles. 'What happened to the disc golf guy?'

They ate their noodles. They filed into their reclining seats in the cinema and watched as, one by one, a group of college students went crazy and strangled one another until there was a lone student remaining, and that was where the movie left things— with one maniac still wandering the earth. Carla dropped Skye home and kissed her goodnight. When she checked her phone there was a message from Nathan, the disc-golf guy.

She met him at South Brighton. They bought ice creams and took a track through the red-zoned land beside the estuary, past wading birds and Do-Not-Swim signs. He was wearing jeans and a T-shirt this time, but with the T-shirt tucked in. He was so clean-shaven he looked waxy. 'Have you heard of Naughty Boys' Island?' he asked. Weird to hear him say the phrase *naughty boys*. Weird to see his tongue graze his ice cream. She looked away towards the pōhutukawa next to the track, the occasional ruin of a wall, the hillside suburb across the water.

'Around here?'

'Up ahead. Two boys got killed building a tunnel there in the sixties. It collapsed on them.'

'No, that's awful.' This set off her quake memories somehow, the same tired old loop. There wasn't much violence in them anymore, mainly aftermath—damage, silt and mud she couldn't trust. For weeks nothing clean, nothing straight, over and over again, relentless. Not now, she told herself. Change the subject. 'They have a good view now, these people,' she said, and crunched into her cone. For the houses behind the track, it was a kind of unglamorous Riviera. There was nothing between them and the water anymore, only this communal lawn, practically deserted, silent as the grave.

'Just sea level rise to worry about,' Nathan said. She didn't answer right away. There was a risk of brain-freeze if she spoke too soon. 'I used to build tunnels as a kid,' he said. '*The Great Escape.* I loved that.' He hadn't mentioned movies that old before. He was going off-profile.

'How? Do you just, like, dig down and then turn sideways?' She looked up at him.

'You have to brace it with something. In sandy ground like this you wouldn't even bother.' He lifted his hands to face each other, palm-to-palm. Shy biceps swelled on the underside of his arms. The track was about to curve around and meet up with suburbia again, hopefully a cup of coffee. 'It might *seem* firm with moisture in it. They might have even propped something up down there.' She eyed the frame he'd erected with his limbs, willing it to hold. 'It might take the earth on either side a while to loosen, once the pressure is released. But it will correct itself eventually.' He moved his arms and down it all came. 'Here, or here, or here. It would have happened instantly.'

Their little hearts going. Like rabbits or rats, bolting for the open air.

'One second—'

'Stop,' she said. 'Sorry. Please.' Her heart.

Emergency Procedures

Until she was twelve Flick went to her grandparents' house after school. There, in the place the internet forgot, the contradictions of her late childhood—lip gloss and bare feet, wizarding worlds and sportswear brands—assumed a smaller scale. The house was wrapped around an inner, concreted courtyard. The kitchen and adjoining family room opened onto that, and there were other doors too. Her grandfather was often behind one, an invisible presence, doing what her gran called his pottering with rocks. There were more doors onto the courtyard than there were rooms in the house, it had seemed to Flick when she was little. She'd carried this with her, the impression of surplus doors, a sense of plenty. She was comfortable in a world of possibilities.

The same applied to the prints that hung in the family room, of an azure bay and a tree beside a road with paddocks stretching away on either side. She didn't wonder if the scenes were real, whether the bay had a name or the road led to a particular town or city. She spent time with her gran in this light-filled room, with its cabinets and drawers full of useful or mysterious objects: used gift wrap and greeting cards that Flick might like (one of a dreamlike white Christmas somewhere far away), empty jars and yoghurt pottles, and something made from leaves of perforated metal held together with screws. The fancy glasses and china were in the lounge, where Flick had to practise a level of caution she found too stifling.

The day after the worst earthquake, Flick, now twenty-two, received a clutching hug from her grandmother. 'I've got my bags ready.' Her gran's voice was steady, at least. She had more control over her words than her body. Flick was driving the two of them north, to her aunt and uncle's house. She could see past her gran into the family room, which was largely intact. Any surviving vases, books and pot plants had been removed from the shelves and placed on the floor.

'Are they in your room?' she asked. Her gran's skin was paler than usual.

'Robert will take them.' Robert had greeted Flick on the porch—grey-haired, shorts with a belt. He was a neighbour. He stepped into the doorway.

'I can—'

'Okay, thanks.' Flick could smell the residue of broken condiment bottles wiped up in a hurry. The aroma was sweeter here than at her flat, less pungent—no curry paste. Robert walked around the two of them with the suitcase, so purposeful he seemed intent to carry it to Amberley himself. There came a distant roar, an accumulation of force, and a fraction of a second later the ground juddered briefly. Her gran's arm struck out and found Flick's. Time to go. Robert stopped, braced, and kept walking to where the car was parked on the street.

Flick had checked seatbelts and put the keys in the ignition when something startled her. Robert, knocking on the window, his eyes fixed with good humour. He was holding something large and flat, wrapped in a thick sheet of plastic. 'Oh, that's to come too,' her gran said. She jabbed indiscriminately at the controls on her armrest.

'I'll get it.' Flick said. Robert stepped back to let her open the door and followed her to the boot. He laid the object on top of the bags, straightened up and offered her a smile of, what, reassurance? He hadn't shaved, and the shadow on his chin was at odds with the belted shorts. She probably looked exhausted herself. She'd seen the expressions of the people in the queue at the service station, the ones who'd got out to lean on their car doors—how their gaze either flickered from place to place or was fixed and didn't move. There were rumours circulating about cars disappearing into sinkholes, about petrol running out, about the Alpine Fault.

'Safe travels.' Robert enveloped her hand in both of his for a moment. Warmth, then the absence of warmth.

She slowed to steer them around a patch of liquefaction and pooling water. When they reached the arterial road the traffic stopped altogether. She inched open all four windows. In came the throb of idling motors. On both sides of the road factories, social housing and showrooms, some with loose or missing cladding, were being pointed at by people in hard hats and fluorescent vests. Her gran stared out the window, breathing in exhaust. Flick buzzed the windows up again and they watched a massive articulated lorry edge around the corner ahead of them. 'I shouldn't have come this way,' Flick said.

'Take your time,' her gran said. 'Is your flatmate all right?'

'At her parents. Where's Robert staying?'

'His sister's got power.'

The flow of cars thinned out on the motorway, finally. Flick gripped the wheel, past on-ramps and off-ramps, driving fast away from the city. She vaguely registered the golden-suede diorama of summer dry hills. Essential travel only, the authorities had said. When Flick had finally got through to her mother in Blenheim, late the previous afternoon, they had decided that this qualified. She slowed for Woodend and Waikuku, crawled through them. When the car's wheels juddered over the lip of the Ashley bridge her nerves registered an aftershock and peaked again. Below, the riverbed was a blur of gravel and gorse flowers.

They turned off the state highway at the old pub, and into the bulb of the cul-de-sac where Flick's aunt and uncle lived. She turned a full circle, realised there was no natural place to park against a curve, and pulled into their driveway instead.

Her aunt and uncle were in Auckland. She knocked on the neighbour's door, declined an offer of tea from a woman with thin, severe lips, and waited in her unwashed jeans with her unbrushed hair in a hallway that was tidy and did not smell of spilled oyster sauce, listening to the sounds of amplified voices from other rooms, until the neighbour returned with her aunt's key and a lasagne—vegetarian, she said, just in case.

They let themselves in. Flick found a light switch and they stared at the luxuriantly glowing coil for a few moments. She turned the tap on to see the stream of water then turned it off again. The light bulb had left an angry red bloom on her vision. 'The toilet will flush,' her gran said, and disappeared down the hallway. There were dishes in a draining tray on the bench and towels hanging on a clotheshorse. A light had been left on. These measures were supposed to convince burglars there was someone home, but they made the house look abandoned-in-a-hurry, as though some disaster had occurred, which it had. In the lounge area Flick picked up the remote and pointed it at the TV. The screen flared to life and showed contestants on a game show. A close-up on a face, then a group of three above a bank of lights. She didn't take in any words or meaning, just an assault on the silence, then she switched to news and her gran came back and they watched the footage.

'That's Cashel Street,' Flick said. The row of slumped shopfronts wasn't familiar. It turned out destruction looked similar wherever it was, and the people were the same as in so many other news reports, wearing their disguise of blood and grit. She didn't cry when she watched coverage of disasters overseas, though, not even when dust-covered children were carried from bombsites on stretchers. She worked part time in an old brick building on Colombo Street, over the railway tracks from town in Sydenham. She hadn't heard anything from the owner. The lasagne was still sitting on the bench where she'd put it down. The bags were in the car. She tried to get up but she'd become a dead weight in the softness of the sofa cushions. She checked her phone. Two texts had come through from her mother, which must have been sent the day before.

Can't get thru you ok

'Is that Louise? Will they come and get you?' her gran asked.

Do you have food?

She'd spoken to her mother several times since then. 'They're trying to book me a flight.' She scooched to the front of the sofa, but her gran was already up.

'I'll turn the oven on,' her gran said. It was only five o'clock, but Flick didn't stop her. The sooner night came, the sooner they'd wake up in a different day. It all still would have happened, though. She picked up the landline's handset and keyed in her parents' number. A text might take hours to arrive.

The bus she was on had rocked—not so hard to begin with. She'd put her hands out to steady herself, but by the time her hand reached the pole beside her seat it wasn't there. *She* wasn't there. She was on the floor of the bus, beside someone's foot. She stayed there, jolting with the metal, the wheels and the legs, hearing cries, they might have been coming from her, she couldn't tell. When the first round of shaking stopped she pulled herself to her feet, tight with adrenaline, using the pole that had abandoned her, and looked out the windows. The driver had brought the bus to a stop.

What she saw was a new reality performing a detailed impression of the old one. Everything seemed to be in its place at first. Then she began to notice differences. Bricks were scattered across the footpath further along the road. The power poles leading back towards the student union building, where she'd been issued with her ID card less than an hour earlier, didn't line up. Liquid silt emerged from several drains and spread rapidly. Silence, like a held breath. Then everyone started talking. One of the passengers, a girl wearing a University of Hawai'i tank top, hugged her. The doors of cars that had pulled over or stopped in the middle of the road opened, and the drivers emerged. The bus driver announced that he would take all of them wherever they needed to go, or as close to it as he could. He lived alone, he said. He didn't have anything else to do. They hadn't gone far when they heard the first sirens.

Flick and her gran lingered at the table after their meal. Her gran watched her. 'Your hair's so shiny,' she said. 'I can still see you riding your bicycle down the road to us after school, so determined.'

'My bike was stuck in high gear. That's why.' Flick pointed to the plastic-wrapped package leaning against the back of the couch. 'What's that?'

'Have a look. It was your grandfather's.'

'Why did you bring it?'

'I've been trying to declutter. Why today, I don't know.'

'Robert brought it out to the car.'

'That's right. He did.'

She'd assumed from the shape that it was a framed picture, but when she pulled back the last of the plastic she saw a book with a maroon fabric cover and letters tooled in gold. *New Zealand: Graphic and Descriptive*. It was big enough to cover half of the small table. She lifted the cover gently and placed it down, open. The title page used elaborate fonts that mimicked branches and vines. In the centre was a landscape—a lake and mountain—in a locket-shaped oval. The level of ornamentation was disorientating. According to a list of illustrations the volume was made up of lithographs and woodcuts. 'They sent us an invitation to purchase on monogrammed paper,' her gran said. 'In the Seventies.'

'So it's not actually that old,' Flick said. The first image she turned to was Wellington Harbour in the 1870s. Wooden buildings clustered nearer the water. In the foreground were a paddock and a couple of cows. She turned a few pages over to a scene of the Pink and White Terraces, like a giant cascading growth of coral with round pools on each level. She felt a faint pang of familiarity. Her grandfather might have shown it to her.

'It was a mass mailout' her gran said. 'I suppose they reprinted enough to cover their orders. We were impressed at the time.'

They took turns brushing their teeth. Flick came across traces of feeling from childhood visits. In the hallway, the strangeness of a goodnight hug from her aunty, both in their pyjamas. Her aunt had used a more expensive moisturiser than her mother's. She dragged a single mattress into the spare room and let it drop onto the floor beside the bed where her gran would sleep. By now, her vision had taken on a grainy quality. Her cousins had moved out, but there were still rows of taekwondo trophies on a shelf above her mattress. They were spiky with kicking arms and legs, but looked to be plastic and too light to cause any damage. The house was a single storey and made of timber. It shared a back fence with the local primary school's field.

When they were kids, she remembered, she and her cousins had found all kinds of things that had been thrown over to their side, from balls (tennis, usually) to wine bottles. A couple of times a child had even vaulted the fence to retrieve something, in the process introducing an entirely new phase of play—the child would call their friends over or she and her two cousins would jump the fence and join them on the field. The town was small enough that her cousins knew most of the kids anyway. There was only the one primary school. Once, the two sides of the fence had opted to enter into a feud and eventually declared a war. The reason wasn't clear, even at the time. There might have been a fraught history between one of the new kids and one of the cousins or both; but it was just as likely to have been random, a matter of mood, arising from a tension one of the kids carried with them that day.

Flick closed her eyes and listened to a car pulling into the driveway beside the bedroom window, the whispered greeting to an excited dog, then a calmer exchange of adult voices, as though they were bearing down on her.

Her gran's breathing was deep and even, like the snow in a Christmas carol. Then it stopped. She was either dead or awake. 'Gran?'

'Yes, love.'

'I'm glad Grandad didn't have to see this.'

'I know, love. Lovely girl.'

Signs of Life

When Tony visited his local Work and Income branch to ask why his payment hadn't gone through, the woman behind the desk told him he was dead. Anthony William Rule was deceased, according to the system. It was a normal day in every other sense. The weather was warm enough for short sleeves. The security guard had raised his chin at Tony when he walked in. 'Definitely says you've died,' the woman said. He showed her his driver's licence. This was all it was good for anymore. He hadn't been allowed to drive since his seizure four months earlier. The doctors said it hadn't caused him any harm. Now this.

It wasn't a question of identification, the woman said. They didn't have the authority at a local branch to overrule a status of deceased. The software wouldn't allow it. 'I'm here in front of you,' Tony said.

'Yes, but I can't change it.'

'Joyce.' That was what her name tag read. Tony exhaled and composed himself. He'd been warned against raising his voice.

'I understand that you're frustrated.'

'Can you prove that I'm dead?'

'People use the obituaries to defraud the system.'

'Show me my obituary, then.' Joyce lowered her head, forbearing. If anyone was bearing anything, it was him. 'Wouldn't you send a letter out?'

'To someone who had died.'

'Can you ask your manager?' She got up, went away, came back. The manager was on a tea break, she told him, but they would attach a note to his file to say it was under review. The agency that handled such matters was Births, Deaths and Marriages—Internal Affairs.

Haunting the bus stop, he remembered a first aid course he'd taken many years earlier. As long as the crew on the fishing boat were fewer than twelve, they didn't need a ship's doctor. But they did need someone with a current first aid certificate, trauma grade. In a medical emergency, the instructors said, check the vital signs or signs of life. There were four: body temperature, blood pressure, heart rate, and breathing. Tony drew a breath in and released it. His heart rate was slightly increased, he thought. Blood pressure, hard to say. The wrong buses came and went. Fishhook injuries—by far the most common—weren't covered in the general first aid course. When the right bus finally arrived his breath hollowed for the moment he held his card up to the reader, but it chirped and the red light pulsed and he made his way to his usual seat.

The bus peeled away from the curb, and the grocer beside

her fruit stand. Tony knew people who were dead. Two had been involved in accidents during their school years. Car and gun. He hadn't thought about those people for a long time. He probably wouldn't remember them if they had lived. The dead had sway, for all their absence. Tony's mother had told him during her final illness that she had never been taken so seriously before. Everyone did precisely what she asked them to do. She was thin, oh she was thin when he hugged her— birdlike, all ribs. 'It's ironic,' she'd said. 'I only experienced the same authority once before and that was when I was in labour. People give you very few excuses.' He couldn't help but try to imagine what she was feeling in the last few days, drifting in and out of a painful mist, a thin horizon of flowers and bedclothes, love and fear. Of the dead people he knew, he missed her the most.

By the time the hydraulic doors of the bus hissed open he was beginning to ponder how he might recount the story of his demise to his living friends. He would wait, he thought, until it was resolved. It was funny. He was fairly sure it was. His wife thought so, when he got home. 'What did you say to them?' she wanted to know.

'I just said, I'm right here.'

'And what did they say?'

'She said, that's not enough.'

'Haha.' It was amusing, the thought of his being dead.

On the Internal Affairs website they were presented with a list of options. His wife took control of the mouse. 'This is where you make an appointment,' she said. They were supposed to tick a box to indicate the purpose of the visit. There was no box for the undead, not at the local office.

'Check Wellington,' Tony said. The options for the Wellington branch were the same. The closest to his situation was change-of-name. 'What would you change your name to?' he asked his wife.

'I don't know. I can't imagine being anyone else.'

'I can't imagine being dead,' Tony said.

'Nor should you,' she said, somewhat sharply. They decided to send an enquiry to the general customer service inbox. God only knew how long it would take them to reply to that.

'I can write something to the effect that you're alive,' his doctor told him. 'No problems there.' Thanks to Tony's diabetes, his doctor knew who he was. 'We don't have a template, is the only thing. I might have to contact someone there to ask what they need.' They being Internal Affairs.

'Good luck with that,' Tony said, while his doctor typed. 'Last time you said I might be able to start driving again, too, if we can prove the seizure was a one-off.' The Transport Agency might think he was dead too.

His doctor was online. 'There's something called a Certificate of Existence. Wouldn't you think they could keep their own house in order?' He had better things to do. Tony stared at the bone model on the shelf behind his doctor's head. He tried to convince himself that under the flesh, his hand was the same as that, and that his innards sat in much the same way as the plastic organs in the flayed torso. As he sat there, his heart was jolting beneath his ribs—electrified. It wasn't easy. His mind was haughty and rejected his offal.

'Can't you just write something along the lines that I'm the same Tony you've always known?'

His doctor swivelled left and right in his chair. 'The same? Not quite the same of course. Your cells regenerate.'

Tony's seizure had been caused by the worst hypo he'd ever had. The hypo had been brought on by a case of the flu he'd suffered while his wife was away on a caravan trip with friends. In his feverish state it was he who was in a caravan, parked in Khartoum or on the Antarctic ice. He'd skipped meals and injections. Luckily their former foster daughter had called, and he'd been able to pick up the phone to form a few slurred words. Everything else was hazy. All he could remember was the paramedics putting the IV line in. 'Hands and feet are frozen,' he'd heard someone say.

Since then, their former foster child had become a young mother herself. Tony phoned her that evening, but not to give her the bad news. She had enough to cope with. He asked most of the questions, and he listened not just to her brief responses but to how they were delivered. 'How's she sleeping?' There was a TV on in the background and the baby was crowing.

'You know—day and night, it's the same to her.' She made marketing calls from their flat while the baby was sleeping, for insurers and office suppliers. The Maxi-Vac cleaning system, which was less, not more, convenient.

'Is her dad helping out?'

'Yeah, of course.' Tony could picture him, within earshot, on the couch in front of the TV. He didn't care much about time of day either.

'Is he looking for work?' A few months before he'd failed a drug test—a one off thing, not a problem, so she said.

'Yeah, of course.' The longer the call went on, the louder the baby got.

'How do they tax you for those calls you make?'

'They just take it out. I don't have to do anything.'

'So you're an employee?'

'Yeah. I mean, I think it's all fine.'

'I'm sure it is. I was just curious.' Tony wondered what would happen if he himself were to earn a wage, his current status being what it was, or commit a crime for that matter. He'd be surprised if Inland Revenue would give up on him as easily.

The following morning, he sat with his coffee beside the phone and watched the neighbour's cat traverse his lawn. Calico it was called, that colour combination. He had done all he could for now. A letter from his doctor along with his passport ought to be enough. Usually, he would open the sliding door and hiss the cat on its way, ever since he'd seen it scattering dirt under the camellia bush with its back legs. He got up and pulled the sliding door open. He had to move quickly or the cat would reach the fence and perform one of the acrobatic leaps it handled with such ease. He leaned his head out. 'Hello puss.' He spoke in the voice he used with animals he was happy to see. Animals could tell the difference. This one could. It stopped and turned its head. 'Hello puss.' It turned all the way around. He pushed the door open further, and left it open. He picked up his coffee cup and carried it to the bench. He returned the milk to the fridge. By the time he'd performed those few tasks the cat was crossing the living room.

'Meow,' it said. It walked between Tony and the fridge, stopped in front of the pantry and meowed again, then repeated itself at intervals of approximately five seconds. They didn't speak the same language, but this creature could convey its message perfectly clearly. The answer to what Tony felt was a demand rather than a polite request was no. He picked it up and carried it, dangling, to the sliding door. He dropped it onto the concrete. Such things happened to domestic animals. Children, too. They could be standing in one place, making their needs felt, and the next moment they would be hoisted up into the air and set down somewhere else, among a completely different set of risks and opportunities.

He had his wallet and keys and was about to open the door when the phone rang. 'Is that Anthony Rule?'

'Yes.'

'Mr Rule. Anthony. This is Joyce Calder calling from Work and Income. We spoke at the office on Tuesday.'

'Oh. Hi Joyce.'

'Um. Anthony, I wonder if you've checked your bank account today.'

'My bank account? What now?'

'I need to inform you that your benefit payments were delayed due to the public holiday the previous Friday. The money should be in your account now.'

'Am I not dead, then?'

A nervous laugh. 'Actually, there was an error on Tuesday. I must have had records open in two different windows. They overlapped.' She paused. He could feel a force rising in him—the righteousness of the wronged. 'As I say, Mr Parker, I'm very sorry for any concern that might have been caused.' Another pause. 'It was my mistake.' He could see Joyce holding the phone, the clusters of bulky rings she wore. He could hear the resignation in her tone. She had to tolerate herself as well as others. Life was a long time in the living. He took a breath.

'So, I can call it off with Internal Affairs?'

'Call what off with them?'

'My enquiry.'

'You didn't have to enquire with them.' She had got some of her steam back. 'I told you your case was under review.' His first response was indignation, and then a small misgiving crept in. He took a breath. 'No bother,' he said. 'These things happen.'

'Thanks.' She gathered herself. 'Thanks for your understanding. Goodbye then.'

Tony ended the call and put his phone down. It wasn't over, not yet. He would have to phone his doctor back, and send another email to Internal Affairs. Or he could just leave things as they were. Miss his appointment. Receive his Certificate of Existence. He wouldn't mind having one.

'I've been thinking.' It was his wife, fresh out of the shower, leaning against the doorjamb in the robe that barely covered her thighs. 'Maybe I could help you establish proof of life.'

Tony stood up—still some blood pumping in there. 'Could you just?' He didn't tell her about the call, not yet. *Ah Tone*, she was fond of saying. *You just let life carry you. That's what you do: go where the sea takes you.* Having been a man on the ocean, all those long hours, knowing its power, he didn't take this as the rebuke it was intended to be. Driftwood was what they all were, eventually.

Brutalism

After the earthquakes, after she'd dropped out of university and after the print shop had sold, Flick got a job with a company that compiled advertising circulars. The office was based on the third floor of a new block. That particular type of building, with a frame of compressed timber, was proving popular in the rebuild, so popular that the architects brought groups of visitors through occasionally—developers, surveyors, planners. They were close enough to Flick's desk one afternoon that she could hear the tour guide's spiel. 'Can you see Sugarloaf, sticking up over there? Te Heru-o-Kahukura.' The visitors, most from out of town, all turned to look out a window—some south, towards the hills and the transmission mast he'd pointed out, some east towards the beaches. The windows stretched floor to ceiling. 'The glass will bend and flex if it needs to,' the guide said.

One face—*his* face—turned towards Flick's and stopped. He was dressed similarly to the rest, on the spectrum of checked shirts, but there was something unruly beyond that, either in the Flying Nun mullet or in his gaze, which stayed trained on her slightly too long (not long enough). Pale eyes. The others wore tentative smiles, as though the guide might be joking about the glass. He wasn't joking. Come five o'clock, tenants and visitors were all welcome at a drinks reception on the ground floor.

He was a trainee architect from Auckland, he told her. They formed a cluster of two in the foyer. Flick held her glass by its stem. 'The acoustics in here could be better,' he said. He had to move in quite close for her to hear. She was stuck in a feedback loop between his eyes and the bulk of his looming shoulders. He was already wearing his outer layer, a kind of duffel coat, which gave their conversation a sense of urgency. In stooped bursts he shared a few of his enthusiasms, most of which relied on new technologies, such as buildings that were modular or temporary. Disaster recovery was a growing field, he said. Responding to disruption: climatic, social, political. He straightened up again. Flick's colleagues, people she ate lunch with, were beside the stairs. She didn't care. She didn't move and nor did he. 'Not many—' He leaned down again. 'Not many people get to see their city being rebuilt.' He stayed close, to catch her reply.

'What kind of accent is that?' she asked.

'I lived in England with my mother until I finished school.' It would account for the duffel coat. When he did leave, it was to go to a bar, and she went with him.

For once the next morning, Flick enjoyed her walk to work, past the traffic cones marking a section of road that had been dug up so the pipes could be repaired. The red bunting strung up around the hole was a safety measure, but to her it looked festive, as though somebody was throwing a street party. His first text arrived soon after she got to the office. She could only see the first line. Are you all right? She swivelled in her seat towards the south, where suburbs fanned out across the dry slopes, to read the rest. I feel wretched. I'm going home for the afternoon. You kept me up.

She typed, Sorry, won't happen again.

He came back straight away. That would be a shame.

'Are you all right?' He'd asked her that the night before, as they'd stalked the empty streets looking for a taxi to take her home. Then again, five minutes later. 'Are you all right?' He'd pressed her against one of the chain-link fences that had grown up around every demolition site and vacant lot across the city. Soon after their lips had met for the first time, each of them had opened their mouths and then (for whatever reasons of their own) paused, and stayed like that. Touching, but still. Long enough for a sweeping arc shot.

Between kisses he'd murmured about untenable circumstances.

The production manager, Michelle, arrived at Flick's desk with a lumpy tote bag slung over her shoulder. Her youngest child came after her in a dragon onesie. Under his spikes, his expression was stormy. 'Hi James,' Flick said.

'Don't ask,' said Michelle. 'Shall we go over BulkMart?'

'Okay.'

'Have we got their images?'

'Yep.'

The office manager had followed them over. She bobbed down to speak to James. 'Would you like to come for a walk with me to the café downstairs?'

'Don't worry,' Michelle said. 'He's fine. Only if you want to. I think they have chocolate fish?' The office manager took one of the boy's green hands. He hustled a little to keep up with her. 'Give me a minute.' Michelle took her bags into her office, beside Flick's desk.

Boss has arrived. I'd better behave myself.

That would be a shame.

Through the glass wall separating them, Flick watched Michelle slide her laptop out of its bag. Her ringtone gave her a fright. 'Hello?'

'Are you all right?' Heat surged into her cheeks. She could still feel the weight of him, leaning in. 'What are you doing for lunch?'

Their fairy tale would begin, *Once upon a time*. Once upon a time two lovers (unconsummated) greeted each other beside the railway lines in a city brought low by a great and terrible trembling of the earth. He hailed from a faraway kingdom and she toiled on a keyboard, nourished on nothing but greasy scones. He had walked across town to see her. Under the sun's unforgiving rays he was rumpled and freckly—rumpled for the same reason she was. 'How are you holding up?' she asked.

'Not too bad,' he said. 'Bit peaky.' Eyes like water. Skin pale. They fell into step, or tried to, until they reached a row of shops.

'Do you want to eat?' she asked.

'No.'

They sat on the bench in front of the bakery rather than going in. A shop window across the road said, *More than Cushions*. Only cushions in the window, though, in piles of olive green, tan, and white and navy stripe. Before the quakes she hadn't paid much attention to the buildings that accommodated shops. This one was a white concrete box. The awning was at least braced, to prevent it from collapsing onto passers by. She half turned her head towards him. She couldn't help it. Her subatomic particles wanted to go that way. 'What style would you call that?' she asked.

He looked down and plucked at his shirt. 'I don't know. Middle management chic?'

'The building.' She pointed.

'That? I wouldn't say there's any deliberate style.'

'Give me an example of something you do like.'

'You're quite demanding aren't you? Where?'

'Christchurch. No stalling.'

'What stalling?'

'Come on.'

'I don't know.' He put a hand on her far knee and pulled

her gently towards him. 'I'm not really into Brutalism.' She shuffled around. Now she could see him. 'I've been thinking about you a lot,' he said.

'Me too.'

'It's bad timing though.' He gazed at her. 'I've been feeling bad. Guilty.'

A girlfriend. She had seemed insubstantial the night before, nothing more than theoretical, like the half-timbered cottages Flick had imagined for his childhood. 'I fly back on Friday night.' He gazed more. For the first time it occurred to her that he and his girlfriend had humidity, Queen Street and the Waitematā in common—music she hadn't heard, jokes she hadn't laughed at. His hand found the back of his neck. 'I didn't expect this.' In the rom-com the girlfriend would be ditzy and materialistic. No one would be rooting for her.

His next message arrived as the lift doors slid closed on the ground floor. I wanted to kiss you. And another before she reached her desk. Tomorrow after work?

Jump to a pub, on a road that ran west from the park. By the time they got there the after-work crowd had thinned out. They were in a lull, with low lights and loud music. 'Shall we grab some food somewhere?' she half yelled. He shook his head, leaned forward and planted a kiss on her lips.

'Where's your place again?' he asked. She was in the smallest flat in a new block that went deep from the road, down a long driveway.

'Other side of the park. You?'

'In town. I'm sharing with a guy from work.' He must have changed and put on the T-shirt he was wearing, which had a graphic of spikes and lines on it.

'I don't even know what company you work for.'

He kissed her again, then sat back and watched one of the servers grab the legs of a table, turn it over and place it on top of another. 'Are you closing?' he yelled over the Eighties playlist.

'Nah,' the guy yelled back. 'There's a gig later.'

She reached her neck out to speak into his ear. He had an earring hole, no earring. 'Have you had a chance to think about—you know, the situation?' She said *situation* with a hint of irony.

'Somewhat. I mean, I've been thinking about this,' he rubbed her legs, 'you.' For a while they didn't speak. Eventually the bouncer told them to stop. The situation was, he was leaving the next day. The situation was, she wasn't alone in her mind anymore because he was there.

He messaged her from the departure gate. The security staff are wearing Santa hats. They don't look happy about it.

She messaged him while she was preparing lunch at her gran's, her phone on the bench in front of her. What does margarine even do?

Texture? She tried to imagine him in one of her grandmother's armchairs, drinking out of a chintzy mug. It wasn't easy. Have your nana lunch. I have to Christmas shop.

I'm wearing a very, very short skirt, she told him. It was actually an old dress—so old the fabric was pulled tight against her chest and hips.

Second thoughts, I gave everyone gifts last year.

Where's mine?

I'll bring you something back.

You'd better.

Oh, I will. Flick's gran made a pass through the kitchen, probably wondering where the toast was. She took plates out of the cupboard and left again. Meantime, all I want for Christmas is a pic.

On Christmas Eve he sent Flick a picture of himself when he was younger, sixteen or seventeen. Lisbon school trip. They dragged us to a Hieronymus Bosch exhibition. His face was slimmer and framed by a neater hairstyle. Behind him, over his left shoulder, was a stone gargoyle. She was on a fold-out couch at her aunt's place.

Medieval guy? Fish with feet? She was scrolling images of Lisbon at the same time.

That's him. Naked people bending over.

Educational, then. She was still in her swimsuit but she hadn't mentioned it. He'd want pics, and once things went that way it would be difficult to bring him back.

I thought I was going to lose my virginity on that trip.

Poor teen you, she keyed. The architecture was beautiful, but reckless for an earthquake zone.

I was even more frustrated when I left Christchurch. Her search had returned images of a kind of castle outside Lisbon, with secret passages, underground caverns, stepping stones over water and something called The Terrace of Celestial Worlds. I've been thinking about you a lot. There's a word I haven't used yet. There were thousands of words he hadn't used. Tens of thousands. Hundreds of thousands, maybe.

Harpsichord? She dropped her phone, rolled off the bed and walked through the living room outside to the pool, where her aunt, grandmother and mother were seated around the picnic table in the fading light. Auntie Bron attempted an Attenborough impression. 'The nocturnal creature emerges, blinking, from its burrow.' Flick jumped into the pool. She let the water spread her hair. She couldn't stand it. She got out, dried herself off, went inside and picked her phone up again. I'm in love with you.

He called her, drunk, on Christmas Day. 'I love you too,' he said. 'I do.' From the patio she could see people ferrying crockery and glasses back and forth in the kitchen and living room. The weather was the same as it always was at Christmas: not hot, not cold, some cloud, some sun. He felt bad, he said. He had to hang up, but he would work out what to do.

The morning of New Year's Eve, an email several paragraphs long. His girlfriend's mother had been diagnosed with breast cancer. Flick avoided the feeling that followed her all day. Later, he messaged her directly. Hello? Did you get my email?

She immediately felt guilty. She was out. She'd been leaning over a bathroom sink with a friend, appraising her hair and applying lipstick.

She stepped away from the mirror and keyed, I'm sorry. I didn't know what to say. The Hollywood lights, the continual bouncing of cubicle doors and turning of latches, none of it seemed wholly real. Where she was had become a sideshow. The friend she was with shook out the messy bun she'd just constructed, with a waft of chemical sweetness. 'Who's that?'

'No one,' Flick replied. 'It's nothing.' She wasn't in either place, with either of them. She was nowhere. She was still staring down at her phone when his next message appeared.

I can't break up with her now. I'm sorry.

For weeks she lay awake listening to midnight cars and a ticking she couldn't pinpoint the source of, in the frame or walls. Her excitement was slow to fade. She walked to work past the stretch where a row of media tents had stood after the February quake—international media for several days, national media a few months. She passed beyond where soldiers had guarded the entry to the central-city cordon. There were no ruins along her route anymore, only absences. New sides of buildings were exposed, their unadorned brickwork and bald concrete walls.

A new group was shown around their floor at work. The glass would flex, the guide assured them, all would be well. Flick stared out the window at a diluted shade of blue. Her various layers of outer clothing were hung on the coat rack and draped over the back of her chair. The season was changing, which meant coldish in the morning and anything up to hot during the day. Social media was corrosive, he'd told her, and wasted time. She'd searched him up online anyway. She'd found photos of American professors, a Scottish soccer player and hundreds of unhelpful strangers posing with mountains or smiling dogs, or in lines with other strangers at conferences. Strange dogs. Strange conferences. Breast cancer, if caught early, could be treated successfully.

She opened the messaging app on her phone. Her vision tunnelled. She typed, Are you all right? Send. Done. She couldn't undo it now. She put her phone down. It buzzed. She saw nothing but her hand picking it up.

Getting by. What's new?

He had replied so fast.
Not much. Instant regret. Nothing to love in 'not much'.
Ask me what's new.
What's new?
I've got a job! Once I finish my placement.
Maximum congratulations! This was more cheerful. A new job seemed settled, though, seemed permanent.
I'm going out to celebrate later.
Why tell her that? Have fun.
I'm glad you contacted me. Guess where I am. She looked up, as though a moving shadow had caught her eye. Across the heads, outside the glass, the sky was still empty.

He was on her front step. He was in her living room. She had no time to adjust to these developments. Still the blue eyes, still pale, still in a checked shirt, but something different. His texts had started arriving mid evening, several hours ago. He'd complained about the price of taxis, and the fact that no ride-share app was operating in the city yet. He didn't seem drunk, though. He walked in and stopped between the kitchen bench and the door to the bedroom. 'Don't you have any stuff?'

The living area had come furnished with a vinyl couch. The kitchen was missing a toaster but she hadn't got around to buying one. She'd been using the grill. Two cookbooks lay flat, unopened, on the shelf built into the wall, like props. Now she saw how bare the place was, how provisional. 'I haven't settled in properly,' she said. It would be inane to tell him that she had been able to see the full moon through the kitchen window lately. They could listen to music (he liked his songs many-layered and melodic, with wounded lyrics) but he didn't move towards the couch. He stood his ground.

They kissed beside the bed. She waited for the filmic momentum to build. They weren't there yet. He pulled her top up over her head. She sank into a seated position on the bed. He sat beside her, and leaned down to continue kissing her. She lay back. He followed her down. After several texts he'd called her. There had been voices in the background, men's and women's. 'Wait,' she said. He pulled away, and she held her face in her hands. 'Come over, or stop texting,' she'd told him in the end. She'd summoned him, and there he was. She had that much power at least. She took her hands away. She was down to her bra but he didn't touch her breasts. He reached up under her skirt and removed her underwear. She kneeled on the bed to unbutton his shirt. His chest and stomach were pale and freckled, but strong. Kickboxing, he'd told her. She remembered now.

She was weightless for a moment. She had to put her hands up to catch herself against the wall. He'd flung her around. There was no time to react before the next thing, which was deep pain, stabbing. She heard herself cry out. Once, twice, three times. Through the fabric of her skirt, hiked up around her hips, she felt the stream of ejaculate land. It seemed to go on for an implausible length of time.

There was nothing else to do but rearrange herself into a seated position on the bed. 'You came on my skirt.'

'Don't say that.' He was already on his feet, zipping up and buttoning his shirt. He was going to leave straight away. She knew without having to ask. It didn't matter, though, one way or the other. Something had gone wrong, irreversibly so. Whatever it was had retreated already, along a distant hallway, behind a closed door. On her bedside table were two small rocks. They were fossils her gran had given to her when she moved in. The crab was partial, missing a claw and a couple of legs.

When he'd gone she got up, changed into tracksuit bottoms and a T-shirt, bunched her skirt up and took it down the stairs to the wheelie bin outside. She put it in and closed the lid, then she lingered there, the soles of her feet cold, in the narrow driveway between the wall of her building and the fence. She didn't feel like going back inside. Instead she padded up the driveway, away from the range of the building's tilt-slab concrete walls, until she reached the footpath and the road, where the night had shrunk the known world into the ranges of streetlamps and car headlights. A late pedestrian approached, unsteady on his own feet. He spoke a few sentences to himself, into a chill he couldn't feel. He was carrying the effects of several drinks but no apparent malice, as he made his halting way along.

Crossing Time Zones

Louise left Los Angeles at eight in the evening. If her first flight, to Auckland, was a dark night of the soul, not a real night but a manufactured one, which passed in a blur of infotainment, muscle aches and brain fog, stretching beside the toilet cabins and combing static into her limp hair, then the next leg to Christchurch was little more than a benign bounce, all ascent and descent, sun pouring through the cabin, korus and kia ora, barely time for water and a cookie before the soft puncture of entering the clouds. She drifted as much as walked along the air bridge, grateful to be originating her own motion. She was on her way home from visiting her husband, who was halfway through a contract advising on soil conditions. When he was a student at Lincoln, she wouldn't have believed anyone who'd told her that he would end up in a tasting hall in the Santa Clara Valley. Six years ago she had moved with him from Christchurch to Blenheim, where the industry was larger. A year later the earthquakes had begun.

Her sister, Bron, hugged her in the arrivals lounge and looked her in the eye before relieving Louise of her duty-free gin and going in search of a luggage trolley. Within a few blocks they were clear of the airport and bumper-deep in suburbia, driving in the sleepy sunshine. She had landed, but was still in the bubble that had formed at 30,000 feet. It had something to do with the dominance of the Christchurch sky, a hundred and eighty degrees of it in almost every direction. Streaks of cloud across the blue. On previous visits there had been chimney holes covered over with tarpaulins in the houses on either side of the road, but they had all been mended now. 'Is Flick at work?' she asked.

'Until lunchtime.' Bron lived north of the city. She had a loud voice, an edge, and a contempt for slackers. 'Then she has to pick up a dress for a wedding.'

'I knew that, didn't I? Luke's.'

'I've got the keys to her flat.'

'How's it looking in town?'

'I quite like it. You can see further. You can see the hills.'

Not every house was repaired. They passed one with unmown verges, unpruned shrubs and a wild tangle for a front lawn. Their parents' place, across town, looked similar. The lawyers and insurers had reached a stalemate. When Louise and Bron were kids and they had returned to that house after their summer holidays, the dahlias would be blooming and the breaking waves waiting for them a few streets away. Nothing in the environment had changed back then, only they had, she and her sister—every summer would bring new fads, new hobbies and new preoccupations, eventually new crushes and new disagreements with their parents, until one summer they were too old for family trips.

She showered at Flick's flat, which was a tiny place in a cheaply built block. She avoided sitting down on the bed and couch, where a curtain of sleep threatened to fall, not gradually but suddenly and beyond her control. She could have helped her daughter to find something better—she worked for a real estate chain, she had contacts—but Flick hadn't asked. When she'd finished, she locked the door behind her, crossed under the tall oaks that ran down the centre of Bealey Avenue and walked up Victoria Street towards the centre of town.

The casino was still there, with its folly on top, like a poker-themed spaceship. The corner opposite had once been dominated by a hotel of angled glass and concrete. Then, she would have climbed steps past the pebbledash at ground level or taken an elevator to the lobby. Now, she wandered through a site that was vacant but for piles of wooden pallets, a coffee truck and picnic tables. The old district court building was off to the right-hand side, where before the quakes people had milled around smoking in their best jackets and shoes.

Victoria Square was more familiar, though the town hall and dandelion fountain were fenced off for repairs. A handful of people were eating their lunches beside the raised lawns and flowerbeds. At the intersection on the other side, disorientation set in again. Of the two largest city blocks, one was a gravel car park and the other was enclosed by a chain-link fence. Behind the wire—portacabins and open sky. She spotted a new signage tower across the road. Of course, Cathedral Square was that way, down Colombo Street, though it didn't look like Colombo Street anymore. She could see the giant chalice in front of the Cathedral, or the ruin of the Cathedral. She'd lived in the city centre once, decades before any of this—before the sculpture, before there were even any nightclubs, when lounge bars had tried to be glamorous by adding disco lights. The social revolution had made its way to them eventually, but she hadn't met any feminists working behind the hosiery counter at Arthur Barnett's.

She waited for Flick beside the barrier walls around the Cathedral. The seagulls were still there, and an Armageddon preacher. The hoardings around the various sites were covered with murals. A condemned car-parking building had been painted an eye-watering shade of blue. As soon as Louise saw Flick approaching, she felt the distance between them more keenly. She didn't know whether her daughter would want to hug her, and when she did, she didn't know how long to hang on. To go from being airborne, looking down on that vast ocean, to standing with her daughter in her arms a few hours later was difficult to take in. 'Are you tired?' Flick asked. She hadn't quite applied her foundation evenly. There was a thick smudge on her nose.

'I'm all right as long as I'm upright. Have you got the dress yet?'

'It's not a dress.' Flick started walking. Louise followed. 'We can stop on the way to the car. Have you seen Gran?'

'Not yet, we'll go after this. That okay?' Cranes loomed on either side of the street. Dangling steel collided with concrete, and construction workers shouted to one another.

'Yeah.'

'Can you try it on for me—the dress you're buying?'

'Not a dress, but okay.'

The shop was new, freshly staged and inhabited by a lone sales assistant. 'Who's he marrying?' Louise said it to the drape drawn across the changing room.

'Penny. You don't know her.' Flick's voice moved around while she pulled something over her head or negotiated a sleeve.

'When is it?'

'Saturday.' Flick pulled back the curtain. She was flushed. Her hair had a hint of the electrified about it. She looked good in the outfit, though. She was spilling out a little, but that was the way these days. The trouser legs pooled around her feet.

'You've got your shoes?'

'Yep.' She closed the curtain.

'Have you got a strapless bra?'

'They make me too paranoid. There are other things. Adhesive.'

'Ouch.'

'It's fine.' Flick emerged and Louise followed her to the counter. A siren, two sirens, wound up a few blocks away, then faded again.

'I always thought you'd end up together, you and Luke,' she said. A look passed between Flick and the sales assistant. She'd said something wrong. She always managed to eventually. If anything, it had taken her longer than usual.

*

The stars were out when they got back to Flick's flat. Flick dropped her car keys on the bench and opened the fridge door for no particular reason, to see what was in there, she wasn't hungry. Her mother removed the thick-rimmed orange glasses she'd been wearing all day—probably a California purchase— and immediately looked more like herself. 'Shall I make tea?' she asked.

'Yeah.'

Along with the tea came a question. 'What happened to that guy you were seeing?'

'Which one?'

'It's like that, is it?' Her mother lowered her head and looked up at Flick as though she were still wearing her glasses.

'I mean, there's been more than one in the course of my life.'

'Bron mentioned someone.'

'That was over ages ago.'

The one she'd told Aunty Bron about had been in Heidi's indoor netball team. Hawai'i-top Heidi, bus Heidi. She'd told Bron they took his Border collie to the beach, and Bron had just accepted that for what it was. Talking to her mother was different, like seeing her doctor or doing her tax return. Unless she could finesse the numbers somehow. 'Why don't you ask me about work?' she asked.

'How's work?'

'Fine.'

Her mother put a hand on her glasses case, which was beside her on the sofa cushion, as though she might like to go back to California, or just see things better. 'That's good.'

'How's Dad?'

'He's having fun. He took me out for taco night with some of the growers. They're all big into their sustainable practices.' Her mother pointed at the fridge. 'Wasn't it Luke who took that photo of Mum?'

Flick had left the print in its plastic sleeve, but it had faded a little anyway. She had walked with Luke to the Botanic Gardens that day, after it was taken. Unlike the rest of the city, the Gardens had looked the same as ever. Spring had been in force along the path beside the river, the trees greening with gusto. She remembered that Luke had been more clean-cut than usual, as though he'd made an effort. It had been a while since they'd slept together, probably a year, and that hadn't exactly been romantic. Romance would be a shift in tone. She had felt a little light headed when they were funnelled into a kind of goat track through a rockery, her following him, winding back and forth around miniature boulders. 'Was this made for gnomes?' he'd asked.

On a bench in a clearing walled by stiff-branched conifers,

he'd grilled her about whether she'd given up on uni. She had asked if she could look at the photos he'd taken. He'd removed his camera from its bag and passed it to her. The first image she saw was the pic of her gran that was now on the fridge. 'Aw,' she said.

'Yeah, that's the best one.' The cut of hair beside his ears was very familiar to her.

'Can I go back a bit?'

'If you like.' The rest were of derelict multi-storey blocks and shops. Dust and broken windows. Scrawls of spray paint. Raw scars. The arcades and shadowy alleyways of their high school years were all exposed now or gone. They hadn't talked much in those days, not about personal concerns. Their bodies were more honest—reckless and vulnerable. 'I've been seeing someone,' he said to her. 'Penny. For a while now.' The bald skin behind his ear seemed smoother and more private than the skin on his face. 'She has a son, Ryan. He's eleven.'

'*Eleven*?' Somewhere nearby a bird was singing maniacally, cycling through its repertoire.

'She's a few years older than me. Seven years older. She's thirty-one.'

'Okay.' Hadn't he taken it in, what the sunshine, blossoms and ducklings were trying to tell them?

'I've been thinking we should go on a trip somewhere,' he said. 'A group of us. Maybe Rarotonga?' A trip with Penny to a Pacific island—Penny in the Pacific.

'I might not be able to afford it.' She'd seen his moves, at parties and in bars—getting the girl talking by making jokes or showing her his latest app. This was new. He'd ironed his shirt and the woman wasn't even there.

'You're working full time aren't you?' He wanted her to come. He wanted everybody to get to know each other.

*

The plastic resisted slightly when Louise released the photo from under its fridge magnet, after however many months of being stuck there. 'She seemed good today,' she said. Her mother, Bette, was recovering from a hip replacement.

'She's always good. Half an hour ago she sent me a link to a group drumming class.'

'The nurse showed her how to share pages,' Louise said. 'That will be her new thing.' She hadn't sent any links to Louise, though. Nor had she wanted Louise to change her flights when the letter from the orthopaedic department had arrived. She'd been adamant. She'd only be lying there groggy afterwards. Bronwyn could help. Even this unit Flick was living in—Flick had gone ahead and bypassed her. Her own family bypassed her. On Santa Monica beach, or showing a home to an overseas client, she could be anyone, still capable of anything, but here in her daughter's kitchen she was losing touch. 'Did I ever tell you, after the big quake I had this dream,' she said to Flick, who'd wrapped her hands around her mug as though she were cold. 'I was at a party outdoors somewhere.' There had been a lot of parties. 'There were people everywhere, but it was dark and I couldn't see properly.' Louise could feel the fatigue now, threatening to take her. 'I knew you were there somewhere, but I didn't know where. It wasn't late-night darkness, but it was dense enough to obscure everything. More like thick, grey smog. There was a swimming pool. Concrete steps. I was worried. At one point I came across you by accident. You were only nine or ten and you were enjoying yourself. I didn't want to let on that I was frightened. I tried to encourage you to stay with me, but you ran off again. Once you'd moved a few steps away that was it. You were swallowed up. Gone.'

*

They'd arrived in Rarotonga in the morning and gone snorkelling the same afternoon. Flick hadn't anticipated the stretches of rock and coral that lay only a foot below the surface, meaning she had to lie flat to avoid scraping her limbs. She hadn't expected to be shifted by the water. One moment she'd be studying miniature ochre crenelations directly under her mask, the next she'd be hovering over a basin several metres deep. She'd had no inkling of the numbers and variety of fish they would see, how colourful they would be, or the range of sizes, from darting electric blue flashes to foot-long yellow flute fish. The fish were shy, and retreated before her into intricate corridors (she would get used to this sensation of creatures retreating: hermit crabs rustled off the path when they walked on the island's bush tracks; the white crabs they disturbed on the beach at night were comics, throwing their claws up in histrionic panic and skittering back and forth in their torchlight).

They got back to their accommodation late, partway through the evening meal. The outdoor dining area was solar-lit, and Flick had served herself, out of tin foil, several pieces of food from the umu she couldn't quite make out. One in particular, in the dimness, had resembled a hunk of cheese but had been crunchy when she'd bitten into it. She'd chewed as quickly as possible and swallowed before she could taste anything. Later, she'd woken in the dark to an alarm she'd set for New Zealand time. Her phone's pulsing light was smothered in her handbag or backpack. She had to get up to search for it. She'd stumbled into new walls and chairs that had sprung up since the night before, wondering where the bathroom was, the window, the door.

Self-Defence

The car park was almost full but the forest had absorbed most of the people. Flick parked near the no-entry sign at the end of the ranger's driveway and took the path around the visitors' centre. It was late summer, thistledown season, and soft spheres floated past as though someone had applied a wistful filter. A stand of eucalyptus trees, warmed by the sun, offered up their scent. Two kids stood astride their bikes on the tallest hump of dirt in the circuit track. Under their gaze she broke from a walk into a jog.

Walking, running and cycling routes crazed across the blocks of the plantation that were set aside for public use. She was jogging the blue and green routes, which were marked by plastic tags nailed to posts, with stick figures of walkers on them. Between her and the first marker was 22nd Avenue, a straight, stony road that stretched for at least a kilometre towards a wall of pines. She settled in under the burden of this scale and the heavier demand on her lungs. On her right was a section of younger growth that looked like a forest of Christmas trees. A pair of mountain bikers passed her, stirring up the gravel. She tried to land lightly on the stones, not to commit, like a Mario brother or scree runner, but beside their wheels and gears her pace was plodding. She scanned the road for larger stones that might twist her ankle. A quail, fleet and upright, scooted across ahead of her. Riroriro trilled near and far.

She arrived at the junction of 22nd Avenue and Hotel Road. In one direction Hotel met up with a larger, tar-sealed access road that was used to carry the logs out, in the other it continued further into the forest. Diagonally opposite, where a track tunnelled into the trees, was the first post with a green marker.

The first time she'd run here, she'd returned along Hotel. Somewhat exhausted, somewhat relieved—she'd turned her head and seen a vast staging area for stacked logs, vehicles and the type of prefabs that were used as offices. At the far end of the clearing, across the expanse of dust and dirt, a logging truck had been describing a broad circle that had brought it, as she'd watched, to face the road and proceed in her direction.

She'd continued on. She might reach the intersection before the truck caught up to her, she'd thought. She would turn right towards the visitors' centre and the truck would veer off to meet up with the access road. The edge of the forest beside the road was patchy—clogged up with gorse and broom in some places, airy in others, where there was ample space between the pine trunks. Either way, it would be possible to step off the road if she needed to. Still. A hollow had formed in her abdomen. Apprehension had leaked into it steadily.

She'd been halfway between the staging area and the intersection when she'd heard the truck's gears shift and pick up. She'd turned to see it still some way behind her, unyielding and relentless, throwing up dust from its tyres. She couldn't see a driver, or she didn't see one, because her gaze was drawn to the hungry gaps in the grille. There were gaps in the trees, too, she could have stepped into. *Not yet*, she'd thought. She'd kept going. She'd turned a second time a few moments later to find the truck was closer still, gaining on her with all of its crushing weight and momentum, which was finally enough. She'd stepped into the safety of the trees and thrilled at the bulk of the truck rumbling past, its cargo of stripped logs held in place by giant steel mandibles.

This time, her third, she turned in at the marker and was enveloped by shade. The ground was covered in pine needles and undulating. Very little would occur here during an earthquake, she thought. Pinecones might fall. She might lose her balance and fall, break her arm. The pain would be constant but not overwhelming. The ground could give way if a fault ran beneath her feet, but that was even less likely. More of a hazard were the roots that encroached on the track. She stumbled on one, caught herself. She was taking the fragrance of pines into her lungs. The edges of this block could be made out by a frieze of light through the trees on its boundaries. Ansel Adams—all space and light between trunks. The track didn't charge ahead in a straight line but meandered. There was something faintly ridiculous about running in a zig-zag. She passed two young people coming the opposite way. They had piercings and dyed black hair, and they half smiled at her in their embarrassment to be there, to be anywhere, to *be*.

She crossed a narrow road. Younger pines, with shoots growing out of the trunks all the way to the ground, and clusters of dry needles at eye level. McCahon's kauri in Titirangi. She couldn't see the boundaries of this section; the terrain was lumpier or the planting more haphazard, or it was too large. A pīwakawaka squeaked and bounced on the lower boughs beside the track, showing itself to her. She avoided slimy roots and puddles of morning rain.

Where the track met the next road she stopped, breathing heavily, took hold of a wooden railing and caught her foot behind her to stretch her quadriceps. Further along the road was a figure coming or going. The song of a riroriro descended by notes and semitones. Rotted logs lay splayed open just off the track, their insides pale and soft, like termite mounds that had been smashed or had disintegrated on their own.

She was well into her run. The ground undulated more sharply in the next block. The track was narrower and weaved around individual trees. Stumps and roots in her path were sprayed fluorescent orange and white to stop people tripping, though some had faded. Like the paint on cars, buses and buildings in the city, after the worst quake. Scrawls to say a building was clear, or a numeral.

She tried to gather enough breath to whistle into the trees at the warblers. She couldn't produce much volume, but she imitated their dropping tones decently enough, then she hit on a stronger pocket of breath. Moments later, she heard something approach her from behind, fast. Panting. She'd inadvertently whistled herself up a dog. She kept running, pacing on the blanket of needles. She kept on, and eventually (wrong scent, wrong human) the sound of its breathing receded into silence. Who was alone with her out here? An assailant wouldn't have a dog, she didn't think. If someone grabbed her from behind—according to high school self-defence class—she should stomp down in her high heels and collapse the bones in his foot. Keys were good for eye gouging.

She could hear the sea nearby. Beside her the forest gave way to flax and dunes, and the pines seemed to grow directly out of sand. A mountain bike trail criss-crossed the running track. When a cyclist crossed ahead of her, they could almost have existed in another dimension. A few moments afterwards it was as if they'd never been there. Or they had, but several hours, days or weeks ago, their traces still riding the loop, heads down, indistinguishable from one another. She reminded herself to watch the ground, to avoid tripping. A blue ribbon—from a girl's hair?—was tied to a twig that hung over the track. Lost and picked up. Her thoughts were surging.

She could be jogging through a pine forest anywhere. In Europe maybe, over gently rolling ground beside a different ocean. She turned right, away from the sea, where the track forked. Left right left. She'd memorised what she needed to do.

Something about blue. A feature she'd seen on a news channel, not sleeping in the early hours. A town in Eastern Europe where Catholics went, mainly Americans, on pilgrimages. There were package tours. There was merchandise. They interviewed someone who had walked through a field where he'd smelled the fragrance of roses, which was symbolic somehow. He'd looked up at the sun, he said, only to see it turn blue and take off across the sky. Her grandfather would have found that funny. Something else. During the Renaissance Mary's robes had been painted blue, which was lapis lazuli, which was rare, and the sky in *Bacchus and Ariadne*. Bacchus raised a constellation of stars into it, to honour his love. She slowed for a steep mound, taking smaller steps, her heart beating harder, then braced to absorb some of the momentum as she descended into the glare of a broad road, which stretched out in front of her to a vanishing point.

This was where she was furthest from the car park. There was a jarring sharpness to her perception out here, as though her contact lens prescription was too strong. The trees on the far side of the road weren't pines but were tall nonetheless, with leaves that shifted and whispered en masse, a tide of bright discs in the sun. She was kicking larger, looser stones now, not lifting her feet as high, growing fatigued. The roads were Apple Bravo Charlie going one way and numbered in the other, only it wasn't quite that simple. The grid was irregular. She hadn't seen any signs at all since the first intersection. She was relieved when she came to a dent in the pines that she recognised—a horse track of stippled sand that lead back into the forest. The running route branched off on the far side. There was the green triangle.

The forest was something else without the sunlight filtering through: deep and cool. The steepest rises and falls were in this section, and the sharpest turns. Dead wood lay scattered over the ground. Flick was an ear, wide open. She listened. Rustling of blackbirds and thrushes in the leaf litter. The plastic ends of her laces bouncing off her shoes. In quick succession she saw a brightly coloured food wrapper, then a dead animal in a broken, unnatural posture, or so she thought at first. It was a log. She'd forgotten her fatigue. Going faster now, she rounded a bend and was confronted by a runner coming the other way, a man in dark T-shirt and shorts, silver stripes on his shoulders and hips. He was upon her and past in a moment, only long enough to drop an anvil into her chest. She couldn't have said whether she'd rather the forest was inhabited or uninhabited, this far from home.

If he grabbed her from behind, there wouldn't be much she could do. If who grabbed her? Anyone. If he whacked her head with something. She'd wake up on the ground. She could pretend to have a seizure. She thought she could be convincing if she channelled all her fear into it. Tense up and jolt. If he loomed over her, she didn't think she could knee him in the groin with enough force to incapacitate. Could she, under the onslaught of his anger, grab his testicles and squeeze them with all her strength? Through denim it wouldn't work. She'd have to wait. She'd have to lie there, conscious but still, until he pushed his jeans down.

He'd call her a bitch, spew expletives at her. From a tension he couldn't withstand or didn't want to. From a sense he'd been wronged or denied somewhere along the line. If she squeezed with one hand, if she could do that—his loose skin in her hand, the repugnance of that—as hard as she could, she might be able to bring the other hand up to hit his head with something. That angle would be awkward, though. If she squeezed hard enough she might be able to roll him sideways and push him off her. From there she could hit him harder.

She wondered what it would feel like, his head under a rock. Whether she would feel something, his skull, give way. If he were dead, she wouldn't need to rush. She could walk away, cradling any broken limbs, so long as her legs were intact. Having killed someone or given them a brain injury. No.

She could hit him in the jaw with the rock, break his jaw. She could jog away. Or run, if he had enough adrenalin in his system to come after her. It might take five minutes for her to encounter someone who could help. Knowing he was back there. Not knowing what he might be capable of. Villains always reappeared in movies, bloodied and bent on revenge. She would need at least two kind strangers—one to make the call and one to be on the lookout. She'd sink to the ground, no legs left, and stay there. In all likelihood she'd throw up.

The paramedics would commend her bravery. She'd sit in her blanket in the back of the ambulance waiting for the police to examine her. Would they still do an internal if he hadn't penetrated her? Probably. He might have done something while she was unconscious. (If he had, and if nobody knew—if she told nobody, if nobody saw, if there were no broken bones or torn knuckles, nothing to show for it—where would that leave her?) But in this version he hadn't. In this version she limped out, with detritus from the forest floor in her wounds, beneath the sweep of a nor'west arch in the sky, with her selfhood intact. Bloodied and bent on revenge.

Outreach

Gerald parked at the end of Willow Street, a cul-de-sac that hadn't been a cul-de-sac before the quakes. There were bollards installed to separate it from the unused stretch of road that ran along the riverside. Beyond the river was the red zone, fifteen hundred acres of it. He turned off the ignition and let the rumble of combustion subside. A voice on the radio told him a new complex of bars and restaurants awaited him in the city. 'Gritty' it was, apparently—Gritty was a theme, like Cuban or Sports. He cut the voice off, got out, locked the door and made his way up the path to the last house on the road. The owners couldn't have foreseen when they bought it that they would one day become frontier dwellers. A German shepherd stared out at him from the living-room window. Gerald knocked on the door, then glanced back to make sure he'd attached the Community Patrol magnet to his car.

The man who answered the door was bent over a walking frame. 'One vehicle will drive up and park where you are there,' he gripped with one hand and pointed. 'Then another one will pull up behind it.' Gerald let him continue. 'It's not always obvious exactly what happens,' he said. 'Sometimes the driver of the first vehicle will get out and wander across there and then the next bloke will walk over to meet him, but on his way past he'll bend down somewhere in the vicinity of the other car's front wheel.' Gerald nodded. The man wasn't finished; he was just taking a breath. 'They don't say more than a few words to each other, then they turn back, get into their cars and drive away.'

Gerald averted his gaze from the older man's shining pate. 'I see what you're saying. That doesn't seem right.' The German shepherd had appeared behind its owner and stood regarding Gerald—friend or foe, offender or defender?

'The police told me to call if it happens again but what's the point? They'll be long gone. I asked if they wanted licence plate numbers. They weren't interested.'

'Well, I'll sit—'

'It was good enough for them to make all that noise doing their training exercises, before the houses came down.' He held the frame with one hand and waved towards the hundreds of lawns missing their houses. 'Running around in their outfits. Blowing things up. Spooked the dog.' The dog appeared to have recovered. Its gaze was steady. 'They said they'd done a mail drop beforehand but I never got anything.'

'I'll park myself over there for a while. Finish my coffee,' Gerald said. 'I might get out and wander along the river a little way.'

'You can if you like,' the old man said. 'Might put them off.'

'They might decide it's not worth coming back,' Gerald said.

The man was already reversing in his walker. 'There are a lot of streets around here. How many cars have you got?'

The sun beat down and the temperature ramped up. Gerald tried sitting in the car with the windows open. He tried leaning on the bonnet nodding at passers-by, most with infants in pushchairs or dogs on leads. Many wore caps, or sunhats with wide brims. He coveted their shade. He was soon drawn beyond the bollards to the cracked and disintegrating seal of the abandoned road, where the willows and eucalyptus provided enough relief for everyone. A billowy haze of green, a hush of stillness and light, lay over the snaking river. He looked one way, towards the beach at New Brighton, then the other, towards the city. A young woman in Lycra guided a buggy around the worst blisters in the seal. She had the high, bleached-blonde ponytail of a Black Stick or a nurse from a soap opera. He glanced at the supple push of her walking away. There was another track of bald dirt and dust directly beside the river, raised on a kind of dyke.

After an hour that felt longer, Gerald turned back to the street. No cars had pulled in. He was about to retire for the day, to knock on the man's door and wish him well, when the bright clothing of a young child caught his eye, about ten metres away on the track beside the river. A girl—she couldn't have been more than five or six—on a rise, out in the sun, nest of fair hair glowing. Then he couldn't see her. He could

88

still hear her, though, or what seemed to be her—a blend of laughter and chatter.

There was actually a playground within sight, but that was on the far side of the river and cordoned off. The red tape was brighter than the faded primary colours of the swing set and slide. The giggle again, almost creepy against the backdrop of the empty playground, roads branching off into nothing, into more nothing, weeds growing through cracks, pointless kerbs and street signs.

He looked both ways again, upriver and down, but couldn't see an adult. The track she'd been on dropped fairly smartly on the water side, he knew, into a morass of reeds and rushes, waist deep for a five-year-old, a challenge for little legs. He put his keys back in his pocket and walked in a casual mosey towards the spot where he'd seen her. If he got to within five metres, that would be close enough to make a dash for it if he needed to. She could potter, oblivious, under his supervision, until someone came to claim her. He still couldn't see her—then suddenly he could. On the road only a few metres away. Her gaze, when it met his, was wide-eyed. He stopped. Smiled. He hadn't counted on interaction. From a distance she had seemed unkempt, but her clothing was in fact quite fashionable, if that could be said of a child's clothes. She was more agile up close, more in command of herself than he might have expected. 'Hello,' he said. She didn't speak. She didn't potter. She stared. Then she opened her mouth and yelled back into the trees.

'Mum!' That was where the other sounds had come from:

the shade of the trees, where a woman stood and scooped up a toddler.

It wouldn't even be his first confrontation that week. In the weekend he'd been returning with his wife from his son's place in Kaiapoi, driving along a stretch of road on the outskirts, past the market gardens, orchards and outfits selling motorcycle parts and cray pots, where the speed limit was higher, where a sign said:

CANVAS

FEED

SADDLERY

No-one had any business on the roadside at that time of night, let alone scuffling with somebody else in the range of his headlights. He saw them, on the berm on the far side, in time to slow down but not to stop. He could make out a man in torn jeans and a woman in not-a-lot (short skirt, bare arms). They noticed Gerald's car before he was all the way past. He saw quite clearly the man's reddened, angry eyes because they were pointed directly at his, taking their measure.

'Don't get involved,' Gerald's wife said beside him. She had no interest in outreach. She'd always been more inclined to protect her own patch. 'Keep driving,' she said. But he couldn't ignore a woman in distress.

He made sure the road ahead was clear, looked in his side mirror, checked his blind spot and pulled the car into a U-turn. He coasted nearer, and slowed to a stop. The engine and the windscreen were between him and the couple, if a couple was what they were. The man dropped the woman's arm when Gerald opened the car door. She was breathing deeply, puffing even, as Gerald got out and took a few steps forward. Strings of tattoos ran up her thin limbs. They both had the red film over their eyes. The man squared up to Gerald. 'What the fuck do *you* want?' Gerald turned his body sideways, as he'd been trained to do when faced with an aggressor.

'Fuck off!' The woman shouted, and straight away she was on him with clawing fingernails and then fists. He put his arms up and crabbed backwards. There was no time to ask her if she was all right.

'I'm sorry!' he said. 'I'm sorry, sorry.' He backed into the open car door, arms still held high. The woman left off her attack for a moment and glared through the windscreen at his wife in the passenger seat. Gerald took the opportunity to duck behind the door. Later he would ask himself what he was apologising for, and who he was apologising to.

'Get in!' his wife said. He could hear the fear in her voice. He registered the murky drizzle that had begun to fall. The nearest house was down a long driveway and half-concealed by car bodies.

The woman hurled abuse at him from where she stood, but her words were washed away by the headlights and engine noise from passing cars. Lives poured past them at speed. None slowed or stopped. The man stood still, watching. When they'd gone, his anger would slide away from Gerald, back to her. Gerald sank sideways into his seat, keeping his eyes on the woman, her scrawl of dark hair and pale skin, until he had pulled the door closed. He hit the auto-lock button.

'Go!' his wife said. By the time he turned off his bedside light and pulled his sheets up to his chin, whatever it was that was going to happen would have happened.

There was an unmarked memorial garden, consisting of a lawn and a few shrubs, on the corner of their street. In the house that had been there once, a man had killed his female neighbour and, later, his own wife—strangled them and buried them under the floorboards. The council had pulled it down after repeated arson attempts. Gerald had been disconcerted—frightened, even—by the apocalyptic glow he'd seen out his window the night of the biggest fire. The next morning there was a charry smell, and visible scorching of what was left of the house's weatherboard exterior. He didn't entirely disapprove of the arsonist's impulse, though. Fire might be what it took to ward off a bad business like that. A few years later, after each aftershock, he'd found himself wondering, *What's happened to those girls?* He'd pictured their bodies lying, vulnerable, in what state he hated to think, with liquefaction bubbling up around them. For a few moments at least, his mind wouldn't allow reason in, wouldn't bestow him with the knowledge that of course those girls (women) had been taken away, long ago, well before the earthquakes—buried properly and cried over. They were gone.

'Are you all right?' The woman was staring at him. She was an adult version of the little girl. In fact, she was the woman he had seen earlier with the pushchair, the hockey player or nurse, neither or both. The toddler in the pushchair was a boy. His brow was already creasing at the interruption.

I'm sorry. He was going to say it. Sorry, I'm sorry. He opened his mouth but something different came out instead. 'I thought she was going to fall in,' he said. It wiped the concerned expression off her face. He turned and walked away. Everything was as it had been before. Green, still, hot. He hadn't attracted any attention.

When he encountered the two men loitering on the river side of the bollards—saying nothing much, doing nothing much—he gave them a nod. He used his electronic key to open the car. He did notice the two cars parked outside the last house in the row, but if he called it in, what would he even say? There are two cars parked outside a house. There are two men standing beside a river.

The Consolations of Reality

By habit, Flick's gaze fell on the throw draped over the back of her counsellor's chair (deep red, alpaca or something else soft) and then the cartoon cat calendar on her desk. 'It's like. This heavy feeling dragging me down. Like I'm really deep, and can't let myself sink down but it's so hard to do anything. Like drowning. Like I can't breathe. If I don't fight I'll die. I have to pull myself out, but I can't. I'm trapped in between.'

'That must be distressing.'

'Sometimes, after fighting and fighting, so heavy and so hard, I'll find myself awake. It's really disorientating. I'm all groggy. It's dark. It's like—was all of that just me trying to wake up? And I haven't beaten it, because being awake is being in a completely different element, with different rules. It's all still waiting for me. I can feel it on the edges, trying to drag me back.'

'We have chemicals in our brains that paralyse us during sleep—did you know that? It's possible for us to regain consciousness, or partial consciousness, without access to our muscles.'

'I don't know if that's what it is. It feels like I can't breathe.'

'Including the muscles that control our breathing.' Her counsellor leaned her head back against the deep red, soft behind her. 'There's even a link between extreme anxiety and sleep apnoea. Have you heard of that?'

'You stop breathing?'

'That's right. The muscles in your throat relax and block your airway.'

'Okay. Great.'

'I don't think that's what you're experiencing.' Her counsellor paused again. 'I'm just thinking,' she said, her chin resting on clasped hands. 'In a waking panic attack you might feel less connected to reality, but at least you can perceive it. If you're asleep, or half-asleep, you don't have the consolations of reality. Do you see what I mean? Your brain can cook up whatever it likes.'

'So this is all my brain's fault.'

Her counsellor laughed and shifted from her earnest position. 'I might get that printed on a sweatshirt.'

*

Flick is in a marquee erected over a lawn beside a historic house. She's one of a crowd that has gathered to feast, to celebrate a union. In the spectrum of weddings, if the back-garden type, with borrowed chairs and open-toed sandals, is at one end, this is at the other—twinkly and densely populated. The bride and groom, Luke and Penny, haven't bothered to blend the guests. All of Luke's school friends are seated at the same table. At the head table, the best man is on his feet. A tiny surfer could ride the quiff above his forehead. Flick feels oddly maternal when she sees her male friends dressed up in suits; she wants to smooth their shirts and take photos of them. He raises his glass. 'Luke and Penny.'

Luke and Penny, the guests reply.

Gretel leans over to her. 'I don't get how that's possible. His hair. He must be wearing a fuck-tonne of gel.' They're near the front, but on the outer edge, where they're less likely to offend the elderly guests. Gretel is slick in black and utterly relaxed in her formal clothes, as though she threw them on when she got up this morning. Flick's stick-on bra is weird enough, but she's also wearing shapewear under her satin pants. She's thinking of taking it off. Everything—her breath, her dinner, whatever she drinks, her conversations—feels trapped in her chest and upper abdomen. One of the servers reaches down with a fresh bottle of wine. Flick is aware that they're tipsy enough, but feels no control over her own destiny. They've boarded the fun train and they're travelling at speed. At the head table, the father stands up.

Luke raises his glass. 'To Penny.'
To Penny.
Luke sits down.

'To Luke.'

To Luke.

Penny sits down.

The head table circulates. Luke is wearing the suit to beat all suits. It evokes not a maternal feeling but something closer to nostalgic pride. He hugs her. 'Having fun?'

'The whiteness of your shirt is blinding me,' she says, 'is my main problem.' So that's fine, and his father slaps her on the back and his mother gives her a hug too, and his cousins will dance with her, and that's all fine, and the thing is—well actually, the thing *isn't*. The thing isn't that she wants to be beside him in a dress of blinding white. She doesn't want that. His Aunty Evelyn rearranges her scarf, releasing the base notes of her perfume, and tells Flick she's a trooper. Flick's phone pulses.

'Are you seeing anyone?' Evelyn asks. Flick picks her phone up. It might save her from having to answer the question.

Are you still there?

She stares at Evelyn's orange lipstick, watches her lips form words. She needs to free herself. She makes her excuses and heads inside for the bathrooms. In the hallway, Gretel is staring up at a stuffed deer. 'This is gross,' she says. 'Smoke some weed? I called my cousin.'

They tiptoe over the broad lawn so their heels won't sink, to a row of angle parks on a side street where they stand waiting with hunched shoulders. Eventually a car pulls in, something old with new paint. 'Zane,' Gretel says. Zane leans over and opens the passenger door. He's clean-shaven but wearing track pants. 'Feel like sharing one?'

'That's a yes from me,' Gretel says. He leans back to let her get in. Flick opens one of the back doors. She's removed her thigh shaper and can move much more easily. Satin slides over her skin. Zane rolls up, lights up, and the car fills with pungency. The weed relaxes Flick, but only to the extent that she is too distracted by her immediate surroundings to worry about anything else. The details of the car's interior take on a disproportionate significance—the armrests, the window winders and the sweep of the dashboard. Gretel sniggers.

'Before I came, I was watching this nature documentary,' Zane says. 'It showed a chase between this family of wolves and their prey, deer or something, across a hillside, filmed by infra-red drone. But really sharp, you know? There's this one bit where the deer sprint across a break in the forest—in the imaging it looks like a trail or track—and the wolves have to pull up, because it turns out to be a road. It's a main road. And this car drives past. Right through the middle of this hunt. You watch the wolves break like a wave. They just, like, dissipate. In the car, you know, there's probably some couple arguing about one of them drinking too much at the party, whatever, and actually they've just saved the lives of these deer. Meanwhile, the wolves are starving. They might not make it through the winter. It turned out the hillside was just above a town, so all the time this chase is going on, the town is still, like, carrying on as usual.' What is this guy going to do after this? Go home and watch more wildlife documentaries?

'Pack of wolves,' Gretel said. 'Not a family. Of wolves.' And they laugh, and Zane sells her some weed and they're ejected from the car back onto what's now a dark steppe they have to cross, with what must surely be clouds of smoke rolling after them.

Back in the marquee the party has loosened and spread out—tables in disarray, people dancing.

'Coffee,' Gretel says. With unstinting care they half fill two coffee cups and convey them only the distance from their hands to their lips, and that is difficult enough. Flick remembers a top tip from her counsellor about getting by in social situations, getting by in life, which was to ask people questions. 'Do you think I should reply to this?' She gets her phone out and offers it up to Gretel, with his message showing.

Are you still there?

Gretel's lids are heavy. The closest she can come to being wide-eyed is lifting her eyebrows. 'Shit, that's enigmatic.' She thinks for a moment. 'Are you still where?'

'I know,' Flick says. A server stops and offers them his tray. Bubbles rising in flutes. A bowl of baubles in shiny wrappers.

'What's this for?' Gretel asks him.

He shrugs as best he can while holding the tray. 'Prosecco and chocolates.'

Gretel shrugs back. 'Prosecco and chocolates.' She takes two drinks and two baubles from the tray. He walks off carrying his disaster of delicate glasses. 'Who is it?' she asks. 'Do you know the number?'

It might not be him. She had deleted his number. 'I don't think so.'

'We have to answer.' Gretel holds her hand out for the phone.

Flick takes a mouthful of Prosecco—a mouthful, holding the bowl not the stem. She looks at Gretel. Hands the phone over. The thumping in her chest is blunted by the weed, but it's there. Her counsellor has expressly said, with no ambiguity: if she feels that sensation, she should stop, and not do whatever it is she's about to do.

Gretel puts her drink down, twists the ends of her chocolate. 'I know, I know! Say this. Say this.' She puts the chocolate in her mouth. She's tapping the screen. She's actually keying it in.

'Wait,' Flick says.

Gretel gives her the phone. 'Right?' She's sent it already.

Yes

She looks satisfied, as though she's solved a philosophical problem. Then the bride is there. Flick has been avoiding Penny, her son and the entire inner circle, for fear of corrupting their wholesome good vibes. Penny's reaching out to her. 'Have a dance?' she says. She's putting something around Flick's neck. Flick stands there stiffly and lets it happen. It's a glow stick.

Gretel gets one too. Now she sees that everyone on the dancefloor is wearing them, playing a demented, bioluminescent game of quoits. She follows Gretel and Penny over and shuffles to the beat, gazing at the floating rings of neon in motion. Blue, pink and green on her retina. She invents dance moves in her mind that she can't quite execute.

When her phone finally buzzes only the hardcore remain. They've accumulated glow sticks around their necks and up their arms. They've become lazy, waving like sea anemones. She can smell cigar smoke from a table nearby. She has to be alone for this part, so she aims towards the bathrooms in the house, but on the way sees the photo booth standing empty, its open curtain inviting her in. She sits down and yanks it shut behind her. She takes photos of herself in heart-shaped sunglasses, in an aviator's hat and goggles, in a sombrero. She looks at her phone. She glances away before the words can coalesce. She isn't quite wasted enough to confuse the booth with the bathroom and wee on the capes and boas and wigs. That kind of thing will come later, in a dream. She will have to remove her pants. She'll hold them bunched in her lap, on her bare legs, before she remembers where she is and what resources she has.

Bickerton's Pleasure Gardens

June walked to her daughter's house the day she was due to appear at the council's submissions hearing. She'd passed the Baptist church and the people with the souped-up cars who flew a Ford Motor Company flag behind the fence, when she heard dogs barking. Someone nearby leaned out a window along the side of their house. 'Shut up! . . . Fuck!' As she approached her daughter's driveway it became obvious that her daughter's dogs had provoked the swearing. Papillons. She opened the outer gate, closed it, and opened the inner gate. They were supposed to stay inside but they could zip out before she was even aware of them. Sure enough, one was at her ankles now—busy, busy, busy but with nowhere to go. The dog stepped lightly, avoided as much as possible the cold crunch of the grass. Michelle was waiting at the door in her bag-lady coat. 'Good frost,' she said. She picked the dog up and dropped it onto the linoleum behind her.

'It's not proper winter yet,' June replied, though the dewdrops had hung like glass beads on her washing line earlier that morning. When she'd pegged her towels up with numb fingers they'd skittered off across the glittering concrete.

Michelle wheedled the dogs through the narrowing gap in the door, bit by bit, hustling them back, until it was closed behind her. 'Well, how are you feeling?' She pointed her keys at the car to unlock it. 'You've finished your prep. The work's done.'

'Did you just step on one of the dogs' doings?' June asked. It was her job to encourage Michelle, not the other way around, and she had, throughout Michelle's schooling, when she'd gone into business as a florist, when she'd got married and, a few years later, divorced. She opened the car door on her side while Michelle checked her shoe.

They parked in North Hagley near the Botanic Gardens, and walked out of the park beside the river, across from the private school. From their side they could see a wooden landing, a kind of miniature amphitheatre, and not just buildings but actual architecture. 'We have plenty of time,' Michelle said.

'Colin might come,' June said.

'Ah.' It was a token response. She didn't know him.

'From the museum,' June said. She and Colin volunteered at a community museum near the mouth of this same river, in New Brighton. 'This is far too shallow here. Why would they have a landing?'

'Just for play?'

'That would be about right. Charmed lives.' June didn't associate teenage boys with charm.

'Did Colin help you with research?'
'No, the slideshow. I can't do any of that.'

To their left, where the river came from, over the road they'd entered by, the park stretched away towards Hagley Ave. This northern end was where they held concerts and noodle markets, and where June and Michelle had once bumped into some cousins whose children were so impatient to get away that they tugged on their mother's arms like bell ringers. She wouldn't do it again. She could buy a mee goreng for twelve dollars at her corner shops without the parking hassles.

The road bridge took them onto Rolleston Avenue, where they passed the iron gates of the school and a stretch of dark masonry, finishing at the basalt frontage of the museum. June jogged the last few steps of the pedestrian crossing to avoid an approaching car. Michelle sped up. Two boys in striped blazers sauntered across after them. On this side was the Arts Centre, what used to be the university. Most of the façade was still covered in scaffolding.

This was a kind of epicentre in itself. Behind the scaffolding was an arch. Through a doorway off the arch, over a concrete step worn down by footfalls, was an exhibit dedicated to Ernest Rutherford, who had made his start in physics there. It was closed now, but June had visited before the quakes. The size of an orange against Earth was proportionate to the size of an atom against an orange. *Atom* meant indivisible in Greek, but he had divided it. June didn't dwell on the chaos this suggested. She preferred her facts to be settled. 'He's in there, isn't he?' Michelle had followed her gaze, but the 'he' she meant was someone different, and 'there' was the Great Hall, further in off the quadrangle, where his ashes were bricked up and a plaque advertised them. Not the student but the teacher.

One block further along, June and Michelle climbed the broad, shallow steps to the council's offices, which were housed in a building that was far taller, and modern. Staff and visitors criss-crossed the atrium inside and queued at the café, indistinguishable from one another. June's submission was the first scheduled after the morning break. In the meantime the chamber, a beige yawn, was empty. All of its hierarchy and purpose was reflected in its seating plan: tiers behind tables at one end, two rows of benches facing each other in the centre for the councillors, and three chairs on a raised platform at the other end. In the middle of this far bench was the plaque with the mayor's name on it. An angular young man in a lanyard led them to their table and showed Michelle which cable to use. Michelle jiggled the mouse and the first page of June's presentation popped up on the screen above the mayor's chair. 'She won't be able to see it,' June said.

'There's another one up here,' Michelle pointed. 'Most of them will have their own anyway.'

'Their own what?'

'Screens. Laptops. They can all plug into the same system.' She was right. Laptops were open at some of the councillors' seats.

In no time at all the councillors filed in with their coffee cups to reclaim their places. June recognised her own local councillor, who owned a dog grooming business. It was him who'd suggested she make a submission—on one of her dog sitting mornings, after a clip and blow-dry, when he'd happened to be watching the front desk. She'd wondered whether the smell of the canine shampoo clung to the groomers, but it didn't to him. He half-smiled at her now. His own beard was kept very neat. The other face she recognised belonged to the man who'd campaigned against the prostitutes who relocated to his suburb when the CBD was cordoned off. He'd been in the paper for something else, some kind of scuffle that had undermined his moral high ground. He had done the top button of his shirt up but wore no tie. Then the mayor of course, who took her place facing June, Michelle and the empty tiers behind them, flanked by her second and third in command. June reminded herself that it was the councillors who were accountable to her and Michelle, not the other way around. They were hearing public submissions on suggested uses for the residential red zone, specifically the river loop section, which extended from the eastern side of the city out to the estuary and Pegasus Bay. This land had been deemed uninhabitable after the earthquakes. Save those occupied by a handful of hangers on—'stayers'—the houses had all been demolished.

June hadn't read the names of the other submitters on the list. She didn't know that already that morning a group of young environmental campaigners dressed as fish had entered the chamber. Most had flopped about on the floor before the mayor's chair, between the two rows of councillors. Two, who'd held signs (DON'T DREDGE and SAVE THE RIVER FOR US) had remained standing. The costumes were very impressive. The fish had stiff fins and rainbow-hued scales, but were far too colourful to be endemic. Before they took to the floor one of the fish had rolled out a strip of blue fabric to represent the river. A clever touch, very inventive. After they had left, one of the councillors had leaned over to his colleagues. 'Didn't someone tell us dredging would be good for the fish?' They couldn't remember.

Nor did June know that after the fish, two representatives from a network of community groups, partnered with Te Rūnanga o Ngāi Tahu, had stood, given their pepeha and pitched for a reserve that put space aside for recreation, mahinga kai, education, replanting of native species and stormwater management. The speakers had urged the council to return the wetlands to their natural cycles and undo some of the damage they had suffered in being drained by European settlers. This group had moved the mayor to tears with a poem spoken over a recording of taonga pūoro.

She didn't know any of that, but she did know, having heard a door close behind her and turned around, that Colin had arrived. He was wearing a sports jacket she'd never seen, over one of his usual shirts. 'Thank you everyone. Thank you.' This was the mayor's voice, amplified, then she was saying June's name. June stood. Start with a question. Wake them up. Get them involved.

'Has anyone heard of Professor Alexander Bickerton?' The

mayor nodded, but vaguely. 'Founding professor of chemistry at Canterbury College, which became the current University of Canterbury.' Several councillors joined the nodding. If they didn't know him, perhaps they should. 'First slide please.'

Bickerton's photo appeared on the screen. He was a nineteenth-century man seated for a portrait, and he looked like one. His coat, though, was thick and appeared to be worn for warmth—more Antarctic explorer than academic. His eyes were sparky. There were other things he would rather be doing; things he felt impelled to do. 'He taught physics and chemistry. He was eventually fired for a number of theories and views that gained him enemies, but in the meantime he bought thirty acres of land out east and called it "Wainoni".'

'Wainoni?' The mayor used the correct pronunciation.

'Yes,' said June. 'There was a time when a trip out east to Bickerton's Pleasure Gardens was the hottest ticket in town.' She nodded down at Michelle. Her daughter was gazing around at the seated councillors and took a moment to notice.

The next photograph showed a structure of rough-sawn wood, a kind of pergola with ribs, in nothing like any typical Canterbury or even New Zealand style she'd seen before. Atop the frame, made of what must have been a more pliable timber, was a kind of flourish, turned up like an Aladdin slipper at each end. A painted sign along the side said *Wainoni Park*. 'This was what they would see when they stepped off the tram,' June told them. 'The eastern entrance, on what is now Pages Road.' Three uniformed men leant on railings in the foreground, dressed as something between sailors and bullfighters.

'This was in Wainoni?' the dog groomer asked. Wainoni had become the name of the surrounding suburb. It was in his constituency.

'Oh yes,' June said. 'Thousands of people used to go. Wait until you see. Here's another gate.' The next photograph showed trellises, banners and miniature towers like spun sugar. 'This is the river entrance. They arrived in boats as well.'

Puzzlement, now, was obvious in the expressions of the faces pointed towards June and Michelle, looking up at the screen, and those attending to their own computers. 'He did astronomy too,' June said. 'Bickerton. He had a theory he called "Partial Impact". New stars were created when other stars collided with each other. Next slide.' She sensed movement below and glanced down. Michelle was indicating a piece of paper on which she had written. *Stay on park.* June frowned at her. 'Next slide,' she said. 'The attractions.' She read from her list. 'They had a fireworks factory, which was a going concern as well as supplying the park's entertainments. They staged mock naval battles on the river. Bush walks. A castle.' Michelle clicked through the photographs as June spoke. Some had been copied from books held by the museum where she and Colin volunteered. Most hadn't responded well to being enlarged. 'He was one of the first people in the country to use electricity. There was a zoo, hot air balloons. There's the geyser.'

'How—'

'Oh, explosives. He just dropped explosives into the lake.' She paused. The slide they were on showed a crowd of hundreds watching Punch and Judy in a box the size of a large-screen TV. It vanished. The next was a photo they might have avoided, she realised now, of a tiger backed up into the corner of a cage. She'd better not mention the panther that had died en route from Lyttelton.

The mayor spoke up. She wore her hair in an elfin style, but it was held firmly in place. 'This is just fascinating. It's a lot to absorb. What a character. Can I ask at this stage, in terms of your submission—you're suggesting . . .'

'That we recreate it,' June said, 'or something like it. A statue of Bickerton is my second preference.'

'Yes,' said the mayor. It would be fair to say there were stirrings of concern amongst the councillors.

'I know what you're going to say.' June was eighty-three, but not frail with it. All of her conviction was channelled into that pointing finger. 'Noise. But you've got the whole red zone to play with. The police went in for their armed response training, remember. Blew the doors off those houses. They got permission.'

The people of the eastern suburbs were owed by the council. Everyone knew it, including the mayor, whose own house had been in the red zone. The roads out that way were still munted. New Brighton Mall was a deserted wind tunnel lined with Phoenix palms, from the pier to the abandoned school. June didn't mind the graffiti murals so much, she quite liked them in fact, but people deserved better than derelict buildings on the main drag and gang chases on residential streets. She could remember the trotting club at North Beach, a post office with pillars and a flag, and the crowds that came for Saturday shopping. Bickerton had thought to test the water quality in the river the century before last. Surely one man was worth dredging up.

'All things considered.' The mayor's chin rested on her fingertips. 'This Bickerton—'

'He wrote books. *The Birth of Worlds*. *The Romance of the Heavens*. A novel.'

'Judging by what you've shown us today, he would have approved of the landings we're looking at building for boat hire.' The mayor referred to her notes. 'The living laboratory scheme, the replanting and so on, wouldn't be so very different to the bush track you showed us.'

'That's true,' one of the councillors piped up—obsequiously, June thought. She looked down at Michelle, whose roots were ash grey for half an inch. Michelle smiled, encouragingly. Should she sit?

The mayor continued. 'Disc golf, freedom camping, drone racing. They're all in a similar spirit.' She rested her hands on the desk. This was far from the most eccentric submission she'd seen since she'd taken the chains of office. The city wasn't stable yet. She didn't need the engineers to tell her that.

'What happened to him?' This was the councillor who had taken on the sex workers. 'Bickerton, I mean. After they fired him. What did he do?'

'He went to England,' June said, 'to tell them about his star theory. They didn't listen to him there either.' The councillor nodded. His colleagues were already typing or gathering their papers. 'He taught Ernest Rutherford,' she said. Bickerton wasn't an aberration, she wanted to say, but a link in the chain of cause and effect. The last councillor seemed thoughtful for a moment, but eventually he, too, broke her gaze. Everyone knew where that particular chain had led.

Leap

Ryan approached Flick's desk at the end of the day. He was all larynx and Adam's apple, a human echo chamber. 'Where's that?' He pointed to the poster on the partition behind her: a black and white photograph of a man launching himself off a second-storey rooftop. Below the man was a brick wall with a wrought iron gate. Across the road, a plane tree, a park bench and another man riding away on a bicycle. A train was either arriving at or departing from a suburban railway station in the background. The leaping man was Yves Klein. She'd found it in a cupboard at her previous workplace, while they'd been tidying it up for sale.

'I don't know,' she said. 'Does it matter?' He took a photo with his phone and showed her the result. Paris, the commune of Fontenay-aux-Roses. The street was Rue Gentil-Bernard. 'How would you pronounce that?' she asked.

'Roo gentle Bernard?'

'I don't think so.'

'It's fake anyway.' The artist stretched into space with his flap of hair flying. 'Um, Flick?'

'Yeah?'

'You're coming to our place for dinner, right?'

'Why?' She lowered her voice and hoped he would take the hint. The office was open-plan. Ryan was on work experience from his high school. She'd asked her manager to take him on as a favour, for Luke's sake.

'I was kind of wondering about a lift.'

'I have to do something first. I'm not going straight there.'

He sucked his cheeks in. 'Me either. I've got soccer.'

She titled her head at him. 'You're not asking me for a lift to soccer, are you?'

'Nah. It's just, I have to get, like, two buses and I was . . .' He trailed off.

'Where are you training?'

'That's okay.' He retreated with his sports bag. They'd had him archiving the files from old print jobs. They might be the planet's dreariest records. No one would ever want to know which mop or sofa cushion had been on special several years earlier. She glanced back at Klein. He leapt, perpetually. She liked the image because it arrested her. To avoid seeing a sprawl of fractured limbs on the concrete below, she had to remain suspended in that moment, in the air with him.

After work she joined a rush-hour convoy that snaked through the residential red zone, trailing headlights in the dusk, then crossed a bridge and met an intersection where the neighbourhoods began again. She slowed to turn. On the far corner stood a dairy that faced, diagonally, the river and the dark expanse. On the road to the right was her gran's empty house: not repaired because the insurance had got complicated, not sold because she hadn't got around to it. Flick pulled over and stopped the car. She'd be in and out. Her gran had been spooked by an article in the paper (which she still read). A homeowner had received an electricity bill for their empty house.

Flick hardly heard her car door slam over the flow of traffic. The temperature had dropped. Moisture clung to her clothing and reached into her lungs. Lights were already glowing behind the curtains of the other houses. The council's waste collection bins, yellow and green, stood at the ends of driveways up and down her gran's side of the street—all except her gran's. She retrieved the torch from what remained of her emergency supplies in the boot of her car. A few winters ago she'd raided the blanket, to cover herself with on the couch. The bottle of water was far too old to drink, or she would have by now.

The mid-century lines of the house could have been charming if it weren't for the boarded-up windows and the forgotten towel covered in grit that lay half-buried by grass beside the path. If the roof paint had faded, it wasn't obvious—there was no pitch to the roof, only a mild rise—and in the gloom she couldn't see whether weeds peeked out from the guttering. She got up the steps to the front door to find it ajar, the snib on the main lock sprung open. Someone had tried to prise the additional metal bracing off. They hadn't quite succeeded. A few of the screws were still attached, but there was a gap large enough for a slim person to squeeze through.

Flick lingered on the top step. She shone her torch into the gap. All it illuminated was a strip of carpet and wall, not far enough into the darkness to reveal the cigarette butts, plastic Coke bottles and tagging she suspected were there. She listened. Silence. If someone was there they were listening too, hiding, wide-eyed, possibly wielding something. She turned and started back down the steps.

Penny opened the door wearing a top covered in tiny, shimmering scales. The carpet in the hall was springy under Flick's socks. Luke was in the lounge pit playing with his phone. Beside him, the flames on the gas fire flared and died, flared and died. 'Happy Friday,' he said.

'And to you.' He poured her a glass of wine, handed it to her and clinked it with his beer glass. Well, his manner said, we could be doing worse on a Friday night than this lounge pit. His beard had grown into a full facial hedge, albeit a neatly trimmed one. His hairstyles came and went.

'There's someone else coming, a teacher. Single.' He opened his eyes wide. Now she understood the invitation, the fire, the vibe. When the doorbell ding-donged she picked up a cracker so rammed with nuts and seeds she wasn't sure what was holding it together.

Penny brought him in. 'This is Dan.'

'Hi.' Dan was solid, or that was the impression—filled out

his shirt, wore square glasses. He met Flick's eye and squeezed her hand. 'That's hooked up to your phone, is it?' He was speaking to Luke.

She half-listened while Luke pointed out some of his apps. The volume of the music rose and fell. He had gone into business with his brother importing sound systems for smart houses. Penny's top was reflecting beads of light onto her face. She had dressed up, but not given Flick any advance warning. She probably didn't mean anything by it. She was just a glamorous person. Flick shrugged off her jacket. Whatever she had on underneath must be better than fraying denim. 'What type of waves does data travel on?' she asked Penny.

'I don't know. Is it radio waves? That doesn't sound right.' Penny pulled her phone out of her back pocket. Nobody in their family could tolerate curiosity for long. 'Microwaves, that's weird.' Dan, meanwhile, was watching the robot vacuum colliding blindly with his feet.

He was a high school teacher. Still renting but looking to buy. Over dinner he and Penny listed off suburbs they did and didn't like. One was close to town but plagued by shonky repair jobs. Another area had an underbelly. A certain street in the south was so pretty, but also prone to flooding. Flick had heard some kind of incident on the street from her bedroom window the previous weekend. *Leave him*, someone had shouted, over and over. *Leave him. Just leave him.* 'I wouldn't mind building actually,' Dan said.

'You'd be mad to at the moment,' said Luke.

'How's work going, Flick?' Penny gave her a bowl of pomegranate seeds. She scattered a spoonful onto her plate—she didn't know what they were supposed to go with—and passed the bowl on.

'All right. The usual. Actually, I've been thinking about going back to uni.' It was the first time she'd said it out loud.

'Really?' Luke said.

'What to do?' Penny asked.

'I might apply to do architecture.'

'No shit.' Luke had dropped his host-with-the-most routine.

'That's quite hard, isn't it?' Dan asked.

'You started doing what, art history?' Luke asked.

'I'm a bit scared of the maths.'

'I know some maths tutors,' Dan said.

'Hey,' Penny said. 'If you wait a few years, Flick might do some plans for you.'

'You can't do that here, can you?' Luke asked.

'No—Auckland or Wellington.'

In the intervening silence, Dan said to Luke, 'You've done well with this place.'

'We had to call in some favours,' Luke said. He and Penny had built what they called their forever home, with a floating staircase and mezzanine. Apparently they planned to spend eternity selling cocaine in the 1980s. 'Where would you go?'

'Don't know yet. I might apply to both.'

Penny twisted the top off a new bottle. 'Is your grandmother's place still empty?'

'Yeah.'

'She was probably hoping for a payout was she?' Penny poured wine into Flick's glass. A payout would have allowed her gran to buy the unit outright. Instead, she'd had to arrange something with different types of mortgages.

'She's finally getting ready to put it on the market.'

'What's the land like?' Dan asked.

'Great position now,' Luke said. 'Looking straight into the red zone.' He was always on the make. If he couldn't marry Flick off, he might negotiate a deal for her gran's place instead.

'Did she find it hard to let go of?' Dan asked. Flick was having trouble distinguishing between the beating of her heart and the bass track—some wunderkind music producer bossing her blood around.

'I suppose so. She spent half of her life there.' There was a splash of red beside her glass on the tablecloth. Not spilled wine, but red light reflected through the glass. 'I think someone's tried to get in actually. A rough sleeper, maybe.' Everyone looked up at her.

'Have you called the police?' Luke asked.

'It's probably nothing.'

'How can you tell?'

'Someone's tried to pry the lock off,' she said. From somewhere on the periphery of the house came a sharp bang.

'The kid,' Penny said. A moment later Ryan appeared in his soccer gear. His muddied socks were still pulled up his calves. He raised a hand by way of hello. Luke pushed his chair away from the table to face him.

'What are the conditions on your restricted licence again?'

'Why?'

Ryan took his time adjusting the rear view mirror. Indicating early, turning to check his blind spots, he drove them from the subdivision where they lived on the outskirts of town, past strip malls and bungalows converted into hearing aid and denture clinics. Between Flick and Dan in the back seats was an acre of padded space. Whatever he'd expected from the evening, this probably wasn't it. 'Did you grow up here?' she asked.

'Lower Hutt.' He left it there. He might not have anticipated being set up either.

Her phone was in her handbag but she felt it pulse. It was Luke. Tough crowd.

Flick keyed, This is the guy you set me up with?

Penny's idea.

Their headlights swept willows leaning over dark water. On the near side of the river the bank had been built up to avoid floods in the king tide. The land was unreliable, bone dry or reverting to swamp. They turned into the uninhabited expanse for Flick's second time that day—four blips in an infra-red black hole. 'Why are we going this way?' Luke asked.

'It's interesting,' Ryan said.

'It's dark.' But it wasn't completely dark. Streetlights lit the rows of domestic plantings nearest the road. Camellias, beeches, pittosporum. They still marked the boundaries of the old sections. The grass was mown somehow.

Flick sat forward. 'Turn right over the bridge. This is it.' Ryan slowed the car to a stop. Everything was deliberate. Brake, put it into park, turn keys in the ignition. Once upon a time Luke's first car had been parked here. In the wasteland across the road was the playground where he'd done his best to comfort her when her grandfather died.

'I've got my tools in the back,' Luke said.

'What are you going to do with those?' Ryan asked.

'Fix the door?'

'We may as well check it out,' Dan said. The two men opened their doors.

'You stay here,' Luke said.

'I've got that assignment due.' Ryan had his phone out.

'Could you work on it here, look something up?'

'What do you think I'm doing?'

This time Flick could hear the soles of her shoes hit the tarseal. Most of her gran's trees had been cut down, but the tī kōuka was still standing, its trunk fuzzy under the streetlights, leaves shuffling. As they started up the path Luke produced a head torch, adjusted the elastic, and turned it on. The beam immediately revealed something on the bottom step that Flick hadn't noticed earlier. Her mind registered disgust before she knew what it was: a feathery lump with tiny, curling feet. 'Urgh.'

Dan bent over and picked it up—dry organic matter, not gory after all. 'Who do you think this is for?' He tossed the tiny carcass into a shrub beside the steps. It landed on top, and didn't penetrate the dense network of twigs.

'Luke—hold still here.' She fitted and turned the key in the padlock and let the chain slither free. In the hallway they met only silence. The air smelled of damp carpet, but not cat pee as she'd feared. She and this house had a history. The built-in wooden bench seat and the frosted panel of glass were creepier, though, in the round white light of the headlamp, like a serial killer was wandering through her memories. She found the flashlight on her phone. Luke was focussing on the wrong things. He stopped at the doorway to her grandparents' old bedroom. 'Luke,' she said.

'Yeah?'

'Did you suggest we come here so you could try out your new torch?'

'Negative,' he said. Once there would have been a bed strewn with unpaired socks and the windbreaker her grandfather wore on his bike.

'Where's the damage?' Dan asked.

'It's easier to see from outside,' Flick said. 'The foundations. A supporting wall has shifted.'

'Is it safe?' Dan asked.

'Nothing in there.' Luke turned to Flick. He looked less enthused now that the effects of the wine were wearing off. They'd peaked with the pomegranate. First cars and first times were ancient history.

They found it in the family room—a makeshift bed, with an inflatable mattress. The duvet cover was floral. 'They won't come in with the car parked outside,' Luke said.

122

'Unless they're mentally ill,' said Dan.

'When were you here last?' Luke asked.

'Before today, about a week ago. The door wasn't like that.' The squatter was tidy. No plastic bottles or empty packets, no tagging on the wall. She wasn't surprised they would choose to sleep in this room, which was the centre of the house.

'Shall we call the police?'

'What could they do? There's no one here.' Dan pointed his phone's flashlight at the glass sliding doors. They reflected Flick, Dan and Luke back into the room rather than showing the courtyard. 'How do those doors lock?' Dan asked.

'From the inside,' Flick said. She hadn't checked the good lounge, or formerly good. There were two rooms beyond that, her grandfather's den and a laundry, but they had no access through the house, only doors onto the yard. She hadn't been inside either of them for years. The empty shelves were too sad.

'Hello!' It came from the hall.

'Jesus.' Dan took a step away from the doorway. It was Ryan, his skin white in the torchlight.

'Why are you creeping around in your socks?' Luke asked.

'I don't have my shoes.'

'You drove here like that?'

'Whose is that?' Ryan was pointing at the bed in the shadows.

'Someone's squatting here,' Flick told him.

'What if they come back?'

'We don't know.'

'I'll wait until tomorrow,' Flick said. 'Dad will know someone who can help with the door.'

'What, and leave that stuff—woah.'

The floor beneath them had hiccupped, and now began swaying. 'Okay,' Luke put a hand on the wall.

'That's quite strong.' Flick crouched and put her hands on the floor. Rolling waves, not fast. Ryan did the same. Light beams from the torch and their phones swung around and fixed in different spots on the ceiling and walls.

Dan went for the doorframe. 'Should we get out?'

'This isn't happening here,' Luke said.

'Still going.' In the position Flick was in, with all of her limbs in contact with the floor, the sensation was like being shifted on a life raft, on vast swells of energy. 'I feel like I'm going to be sick.' Her phone was a tiny electronic beacon beside her hand. She waited for it to be over, this latest thing.

'Could be Wellington?'

'It could be offshore.' After thirty seconds or so she thought it might have stopped, but she couldn't quite tell. She tapped her screen. It was just after midnight. 'Where was it?' Ryan asked.

'Don't know yet,' Luke said, watching his phone. 'Still waiting.' Another sway.

'Where's the supporting wall you talked about?' That was Dan.

'North of here,' Luke said. 'Hard to tell, exactly. Seven point eight? That can't be right.' In Flick's mind, a high-speed playback of the road north, its rocks and tunnels, river mouths and breaking waves. Her nerves had picked the movement up and were feeding it back to her still.

Acknowledgements

My thanks go to the University of Canterbury Te Whare Wānanga o Waitaha, where I held a residency in 2020, in particular the English Department and the teams behind the CEISMIC Canterbury Earthquake Digital Archive and Red Zone Stories website.

Thanks to everyone at Te Herenga Waka University Press, including Fergus Barrowman and Anna Knox, for her skill and her confidence in my work. Thanks also to Todd Atticus for his cover design.

Thank you to the people who read these stories, together or individually, in early and later versions—Anna Rogers, Brindi Joy, Celia Coyne, David Coventry, Frankie McMillan, Rose Collins, and Zoë Meager. Ruth and Sophie, love and gratitude to you.

I'm grateful for my family and friends in this and everything I do. Special thanks to my parents Mel and Marleen Head for their support.

I'd also like to acknowledge the people who lived in Ōtautahi Christchurch and nearby in 2010 and 2011, who overcame so much to simply continue with their lives.